Chapter One

10 short stories by
Simon James

First published in the UK by Lulu Press Inc., 2013

ISBN 978-1-291-30497-8

This book is dedicated to Hannah Williams

I love you more than Spider-Man

Contents

Introduction

You hold in yours hands *Chapter One*, my first published book and a collection of ten short stories. Unlike most compilations, this book contains a complete range of genres, styles and themes. Tragic and comic, sci-fi and horror, fantasy and fable, I've tried to make it as varied as possible in its content. As *Chapter One* does not have a very specific target audience, (I know, I'd have no chance on The Apprentice) hopefully it contains something for everyone to enjoy. No doubt there'll be stories that are not to some people's taste, and for that I can only apologise. Or just call you fussy.

The book is called *Chapter One* not only because it is the first "chapter" in my published endeavours, but because a lot of the stories can be seen as an opening. While they are all self-contained, about half of them could also act as the beginning of something bigger.

Chapter One was not written to generate a profit, but as an experiment to see what works, and I would be more than appreciative of any feedback you had to offer. If there are any stories you would like to see taken further in the next chapter (whatever form that may take), I would be very grateful to know. Equally, if there are any characters, genres etc. you think I should never touch again, I would like to know that too. If you are kind enough to help me decide what happens next, you can send an email to chapterone@simon-james.info .

I've not won an Oscar (or even made any money yet), so I'm not going to thank a long list of people who may have influenced the book in some way. (There's plenty of time for that later – at the back there is an in-depth commentary for each story.) However, I do want to show my appreciation to all of my English teachers from The County High School Leftwich and Sir John Deane's College for their continuous support and encouragement which led to this point. A huge thank you also has to go to Sam Dagnall for his guidance on my "short" story *Silver Skin* which he published in *The Hat Never Comes Off*, a compilation of short stories in 2008 which vastly improved my writing technique and made me determined to publish a whole book myself.

I need to thank my girlfriend Hannah for creating such a brilliant cover. She read all of the stories and came up with several great ideas, but this one seemed the most striking. What does it represent? Is the monkey a sailor? A pilot? A soldier? You'll have to wait and see.

The biggest thank you though has to go to my parents. They have both made my life sufficiently easy so I've had the time (and an amazing laptop) to write them, and encouraged me with everything that I've done. I want to thank my dad in advance for helping me distribute *Chapter One* to both general readers and people that may be interested in employing me in the future. As someone who could sell water to a drowning man, he has said he'll help me get it out there, and I know that he'll put every effort into making it a success, as he does with everything.

It's my mum though who has been the biggest help at this point. She is the only person I show all of my stories to once they're done, and can always find a mistake that I have missed, or think of a way to improve them. She's completely honest and very constructive. Not only has she helped me edit *Chapter One*, but any work I've ever done throughout my life that I needed help with. I can't thank you enough Mum.

My final thank you goes to you for buying this. Or for borrowing someone else's copy, and if this is the case, I don't blame you – it's a recession. (According to some people anyway). Seriously, whether I know you or not, your support in this experiment is highly appreciated.

Now on with the show.

Nobody Important

CARLEY: I can't believe I'm actually going to see you!

ROSIE: OMG I know! It'll be great to finally meet someone else with real taste in music!

CARLEY: OK, I'll meet you where we said tomorrow at 9. Are you sure your parents will be alright with you coming out so late?

ROSIE: Yeah it'll be fine. I'll wear a bright pink hoodie so you'll know it's me.

CARLEY: OK, I'll wear my new green one ☺ see you tomorrow xxx

Carley is offline

It was done. "Rosie" switched the computer off, failing to resist the urge to grin at the newly confirmed activities for the following evening – he had finally decided to go through with it after years of indecision, and now nothing would stop him.

Stuart had a shave, cleaned his teeth and

got into bed; he had a long day tomorrow – an eight hour shift at the office. But it was the image of what would happen afterwards that burned in his mind as he struggled to get to sleep.

*

He had been in the alleyway for fifteen minutes. A strong wind was directly channelled to him from one end, so he had become numb with cold. After a while, it was hard to tell whether he was shaking because of the chill or through nervousness, but a safe bet would have been a combination of the two.

Stuart had always imagined the alley opposite Little Joey's Fish Bar to be a quiet place on an October night, but perhaps he had been wrong... It was at Stuart's end of the alleyway that he expected the green-hoodied young girl to appear from, but he was sure that at the other end, by the bins, there was someone else present. It was hard to tell for sure, but quick glances told him that beneath the moonlight there was a tall figure slumped against the wall, almost completely hidden in shadow.

The town's problem with the homeless had

been growing worse over recent years, so it was no surprise to him that someone seemed content in coasting around the bins at an hour like this – it could almost be described as commonplace. It did, however, cause a problem: even the homeless might have a tendency towards heroics. He would have to be quick to the van.

Stuart had no time for any more thoughts on it though, as a second anomaly entered the scene. A slender, teenage brunette began to walk towards him from the other end of the alleyway, but it couldn't have been Carley; she was wearing a red cardigan and walking with purpose – it didn't look like she was planning on stopping to meet anybody.

Indecision arose... Was she a new, easier alternative? A target was a target, surely? But then all that preparation would have gone to waste – this was too easy wasn't it? *No! It's getting late anyway; she's not even turning up! You're sweating as it is, cut your losses and–*

In an instant, the tides turned. Stuart had almost forgotten about the stooped figure that was now bounding from the shadows towards the new arrival, with pace despite his heavy build.

The girl let out a scream only to be interrupted by the man's hand which covered her mouth. His other hand held her close towards him, and it seemed any struggle she tried to put up was fruitless beneath his bulging arm.

The man spoke – a cruel, mocking rasp that fit his exterior perfectly: "So, let's talk about Frank Sinatra then, as promised..." He pushed her violently so that her back rested on the wall of the alleyway, and sneered into her terrified eyes. "I have to say Rosie, I think this jumper's more *red* than pink..."

Realisation hit. This man was who Stuart had arranged to meet with – Carley was just as real as Rosie was. This girl, the only person involved in the situation who was completely innocent, was about to have her life scarred because of the pursuits of two men masquerading as teenage girls.

Stuart didn't know what to do as he witnessed the beginnings of a process that had been gnawing at the back of his mind for years. Somehow it wasn't like he had imagined it:

She was horribly powerless as the man held her down and started ripping at her clothes... This wasn't right, surely? But it was no different from exactly what he had been planning to do himself...

He did not feel a conscious decision form in his head, but one must have; everything became such a blur that he didn't know exactly what was happening, but there was a significant pain in his knuckle and a simultaneous cracking noise, followed by a scream. Then everything was clear again, his fist was throbbing and the man had run off into the night, clutching his bleeding face.

The girl stared at Stuart, paralysed with fear.

He made his move.

*

He looked at her across the van, and saw the sweat running off her forehead and down her cheeks. She was still shaking uncontrollably and he didn't have to look at her to know how heavily she was breathing – it was all that could be heard above the engine.

"How are you feeling?" he asked her

gently.

"I'm… I'm ok. I still can't believe how close… if you'd been just a few seconds later, I…"

She was in tears again. They streamed down her face like a river, meeting the sweat on her chin.

"But I wasn't," he said, trying to assure her. "And you're fine. You're going to go into the police station now, tell them exactly what happened, and they'll try and catch that… man. But he's not coming back. He didn't even know who you were."

"He seemed to *think* he did," she sniffed, staring out of the window. "But… I didn't understand what he was saying – it was like he thought I was someone else."

Stuart said nothing.

"What if he keeps looking and he finds her? Whoever he thought I was??"

There was panic in her voice now, and the tears were persistent.

"He won't," Stuart said. "He was probably insane."

"But how do you know?"

16

"I know. I just know."

Nothing else was said for the rest of the journey, the silence filled with her gradually steadying breath. Stuart repeated the instructions as they turned the final corner and slowed to a stop outside the station.

"Aren't you coming in with me?" she asked worriedly.

"I really can't. I have somewhere I need to be." Anywhere but there.

"OK. Well... thank you. I can't thank you enough for what you've done for me tonight."

She picked up her bag and got out of the van.

Just before she closed the door, she turned and said "I never even caught your name! Who are you?"

"I'm nobody important," he replied.

As the door closed and he pulled away, Stuart vowed to spend the rest of his life making sure that was true.

Subjective Groaning

Do you ever think about what you'd do if there was a zombie epidemic?

I do.

It's probably not something I should admit, let's face it. Football and sex are the standard thoughts bubbling inside the cranium of a teenage male. I have room for those too mind, but I don't think either topic really tells you a lot about yourself, other than the team you were brought up to like or which female features augment you downstairs. Zombie epidemics however, I've come to find, can be pretty revealing when it comes to finding out what makes someone tick.

You're in history, studying the Cold War and wham! – Russian propaganda vanishes from your mind and is replaced by the notion of an airborne virus which transforms everyone with blood type AB positive into mindless monsters, hungry for blood. Your blood.

Scary, isn't it? So surely it's worth thinking

about what you'd do, for when the time comes…

Personally, I think it all boils down to priorities (and this is where you find out all that mushy stuff about yourself that you never even knew existed); what have you always hoped to get out of life? Because when the zombie epidemic strikes, said life will probably not last a lot longer, so you need to grab your ambition by the throat and bite its head off, before you become a zombie's ambition and it does exactly the same to you.

So what'll it be? Something awesome? Something no one will ever forget? The examples are endless... maybe just throwing your head teacher into a horde of the creatures would be a perfectly satisfying conclusion to your time on earth?

Before you decide though that this is how you want to conclude your time as part of a society on the brink of termination, you need to have a little think: will killing Mr Crosswell really be that fulfilling, knowing that in a day or so, the world will have no intelligent life to remember it and show you the respect you deserve? Would anything?

Some people's long term desire is to shag that "if-only" girl. If so, why not find her before the uglies get hold of you, and make like a dog does to your leg before it's had the snip? But will *that* really be as great as you've already imagined? Think about it: surely half the attraction to off-limit sex is the bragging about it afterwards. The breaking of the news to her boyfriend, shortly followed by your nose. Once the zombies get hold, there'll be no one to tell, so what would be the point?

Or has that always been the case anyway? Whether its zombies, testicular cancer, or old age, we're all going to see the pearly gates at some point or another, so what's the point in having any real aspirations in life? Why not just chill and watch the world grow old?

This is how I thought once, but then things changed:

I met my dad for the very first time on my eighteenth birthday. I was in the Fox and Barrel with my friends enjoying my first legal drop of ale when he walked in, a cigarette protruding from his mouth, dragging a grey cloud across the room. He had a subtle grin across his face, as if chuckling to himself that he had missed every single second and pay-out of my upbringing, instead of showing remorse for the eighteen years lost.

"Andy?" (That's me by the way. Hi.)

"Yeah?"

"Happy birthday Son."

"...Son?"

"Yeah... I'm your dad."

The first meeting with my father, in front of an entire pub? There was nothing personal, nothing even remotely heart-warming about it. So wooden, so forced. It felt like he wasn't here to see me at all, but had some other motive he was keeping hidden. But not for long:

"Listen, I didn't wanna come to you before now because it wasn't fair. You weren't an adult. You couldn't be expected to help your old man out. But you're a grownup now so I know you'll understand.

"Basically, I've got into a bit of trouble this last year or so. Borrowed money from... the wrong types of people. Got a nasty man on my back now who won't take no for an answer for much longer. Thought you might be able to do me a bit of a borrow...?"

I stood up from where I was sat. I felt myself go hot under the collar and my fists clench by my sides. My friend Tommy stood up too and put his hand on my shoulder. "Calm down mate," he said. "Not here." I didn't move. I didn't know what to do. I didn't know what to say.

"I think you'd best leave," Tommy said to my dad, his voice brimming with loyal aggression.

"Yeah... ok," my newfound father said, although he barely moved, clearly reluctant. "Here's my number if you change your... if you want to get in touch."

He handed me a scrap of paper from his coat pocket which already had a number written on in scratchy black ink.

It was this meeting, juxtaposed with my previously zombie-like attitude towards life, which gave me a reason to *not* just watch the world go by. As soon as he left the pub, I knew: I wanted to be a dad. I wanted to be a dad and I wanted my kids to know and be proud of who their father is. Is it ironic that a potential future of emotionless, indecisive creatures caused me to discard my own indecisive emotionlessness and focus on a future I want?

No. What's ironic is that as soon as I decided I *wanted* to be a dad, I went about something that would almost definitely guarantee it would never happen.

I knew what my mum had been through whilst I was growing up. Struggling to hold three jobs to try to pay off the debts *he* had left her with whilst putting enough food on the amalgamation of wood which we called a table. I also knew that if he hadn't left her as soon as the blue line appeared on the small square window, she'd not have had to work more hours than there were in the day, and would have had time to stop and just appreciate life for a minute.

I like to think it was this, and not some selfish bitterness of a fatherless childhood, that made me follow my dad after he left me with an insultingly casual handshake and got the bus home. Following a vehicle three times as big as ours was surprisingly difficult, not helped by the road rage we created for the simple "mistake" of driving in a bus lane.

"Don't do it mate," I remember Tommy saying as I lifted my feet from the inch of crap that littered the bottom of his car, opened the door and got out. "Yes, he's a complete dick. Yes, him leaving your mum when she got pregnant made it hard for her big time. But you'll be ten times worse than the bastard if you kill him."

"And ten times happier."

"Prison got a lot nicer since I left then? 'Cause I don't remember it being all that fun."

I didn't reply. I knew he was right, but it didn't change a thing – I'd made my mind up. My dad didn't deserve to live another day, and I was going to make sure he didn't leave the flat outside of a body bag.

"Why don't you sleep on it mate?" Tommy asked. "You've only had half an hour to think it through."

My reply was something stupid about wanting my eighteenth to go out with a bang. He shook his head and drove off. I knew I'd offended him, as if I'd never listened to him go on about how prison was the worse three months of his life. But this wasn't about him. It was about my scumbag of a father.

Whether I was actually going to do it, I didn't really know. A couple of years ago, I remember trying to read *Fear And Loathing In Las Vegas* on my bed whilst being distracted by an incredibly loud, energetic fly. After a serious hunt around the room, I'd finally managed to hit it with the bottom of box of Kleenex. I mustn't have hit it hard enough though because the small squashed mess on my bed was still twitching slightly – I'd not completely finished it off. A few seconds into staring at the insect, I began having an extremely traumatic out-of-body experience, imagining I *was* the fly. I was whizzing around contentedly for a second before having my arse crushed through my own head for simply being there, just as I'd done to him. I then couldn't decide whether to put the poor bugger out of his misery or let him have as long as he could in the land of the living, in case his life was flashing before his eyes and I went and spoilt that for him too.

Luckily, I'm over the guilt stage now and

tend to worry about zombies instead. My ridiculously elaborate anecdote still serves a point though: How could I kill my own father if I had struggled to end something smaller than a pea?

I was trying not to think that far ahead as I walked towards the door of the block of flats we had watched him enter. Yes, I had murderous intent running around my platelets, but for all I knew when I got up there I might have ended up flicking the kettle on. If you haven't noticed, indecision is a common theme when it comes to my general time being awake. It's in my dreams that I'm a decisive warrior.

One unbelievably long walk from the car, and now the biggest anti-climax since *The Matrix Revolutions*: the door was locked. That was it. I couldn't ring the buzzer and tell my dad I was on the way up to escort him through a window, and if I broke in someone would see me before I'd found his room, so it looked like my murder attempt had been foiled by a simple lock. What had I even been *expecting*?

I took a step back and began to scour the building for any other entrance. A drainpipe looked dangerously wobbly, and my spider-senses weren't particularly tingly today.

Just before reaching into my pocket for my phone to ask Tommy to do that 180° spin he was always bragging about and come and pick me up, the door to the flats flew open and a man dressed in black sprinted out of them and away down the street. Now, usually I would have been inclined to get a better look at him to work out why he was in such a rush, but I can recognise an opportunity when I'm presented with one, so I dived behind the swinging door.

It was not particularly graceful, but it worked. I'd cleared a pretty big distance in the time it had taken to nearly close shut, and I found myself wishing that someone was recording my life for future generations to admire.

Having looked at what room number was next to his name, I began to climb the stairs in search for number 18, trying to find the clever comment linking his room number to my birthday.

The place was so normal; it didn't feel right. My selfish, evil father lived here, and there was nothing untoward? No booby traps? No monsters...?

Ah. Spoke too soon.

As I turned onto the next corridor, my zombie epidemic solutions suddenly didn't seem to be such a waste of time. One hand outstretched, blood dripping from a gaping mouth which was letting out a low moaning sound, my dad stumbled towards me – the perfect physicalisation of a zombie if ever there was one. His eyes hadn't changed from an hour ago though – I always thought they'd go red or roll back into their sockets. That was a disappointment.

I noticed that his other hand was clutching a black piece of plastic that seemed to be jutting up through his ribcage and T-shirt. A blade handle. I rushed towards him and he put his outstretched hand on my shoulder so that I took most of his weight. The blood gargling from his mouth was excessive, but nothing compared to the rapidly expanding crimson circle in the centre of his torso.

I laid him gently on the carpeted floor whilst I decided what to do. Should I take the knife out? I remember vaguely someone telling me if you do that the flesh collapses into the wound and the victim just loses more blood, but most of the people I hang around with think that Michael Jackson is still alive, so the reliability of this claim is up in the air.

He pulled me down towards him and I noticed he was trying to talk to me. "I guess that's what... happens when you don't pay your... debts," he muttered feebly.

Things began to fall into place like a vicarious episode of Sherlock. The guy running out of the building who had let me in must have been the loan shark my dad had owed money to, and had just been back to show other customers what happened if you didn't pay up.

I stood up to begin the chase – he couldn't have gotten that far, but I was pulled down again by the edge of my T-shirt. My dad looked up at me curiously. Red blood was spilling from the corners of his lips now – he didn't have long.

"I'm sorry Andy..." he gargled.

A large red bubble filled his mouth, reminding me disturbingly of Hubba Bubba chewing gum, and burst, spattering his whole face. The final movement was one of his eyes rolling back in his head, but it was not what I'd hoped for. I've decided it's not as fun when the dead are... dead.

The next bit was the most shocking. Well, not quite, but it wasn't expected: tears were creeping from my eyes and dripping down my nose onto his face. Now, my memory isn't great, but I'm sure I'd actually gone in there to convert him into the... less energetic state he was in now, but now that someone had beaten me to it, I was getting upset? What was wrong with me? I had hated this man and his absence all my life. I should have been placing a bulk order for some party poppers right about now.

When I got home from the police station after making the statement, I rang Tommy up and told him he was dead. I purposely left out the fact that I hadn't killed him, just to scare him. Even in times like this, messing with people's heads is fun.

"Shit! I didn't think you'd actually do it you nutter! You're gonna get arrested man! And I drove you there!! I can't go back to prison! Shit, shit, shit!"

"Tommy, he was already dying when I got there. Some loan shark, or someone who he owed money to, killed him."

A huge sigh of relief. "Oh. Oh thank ****. Thank **** for that. Jesus... But he's still dead though. You'd only known him a day. Shit. What you gonna do now man?"

What *was* I going to do now? A week after my dad had died, and I didn't even know exactly how I felt. I definitely felt cheated out of something. Cheated out of having a dad, in the past or future? Cheated out of being the one to kill him? Cheated out of knowing what I felt cheated about? Ahh... paradox.

I hoped it wasn't the second one. The official statement inside my head was that I wouldn't have killed him had I gone up there, but now I would never know for sure if that was true. There'd always be a lingering guilt inside me over the homicide that I could have committed. Should potential murderers be convicted, to stop them committing what they had once planned? I don't actually know what the law states about sentencing people who were planning on killing someone but got pipped to the post, but I'm in no hurry to find out.

I had not lost sight however of my initial reasons for wanting him dead. On self-righteous days it was easy to see how my fatherless childhood could have psychologically deprived me into wanting revenge for a fatherless childhood – a convoluted vicious circle that I could happily convince myself my father was completely responsible for. But on other days, his last poignant (and slightly clichéd, let's be honest) words of acknowledgment that he had not paid his debts repeated themselves through my head like a scratched CD, and an eighteen year old was reduced to tears once more.

The one good thing you might have expected to have come out of this whole ordeal, the neglect of my nihilistic attitude towards life and my aspiration of becoming a father, was already wavering. Originally, I was to be the perfect dad: a fountain of wisdom and advice with a substantially innocent past to refer to, brimming with the self-respect required to gain admiration from any child. But the more I thought about it, the less realistic this aspiration seemed to be: How was it possible if I knew that I had been planning to kill someone? Would that snippet of information be one I would share with Mini-Me, or would I lie by omittance and fail to mention it, knowing deep down that I was not fit to bring up a hamster, let alone a human being?

So I pretty much fell back into my initial way of thinking... Watching the world go by was so much easier than actively going about trying to become a father. The only thing I could perhaps still hope for was a zombie epidemic, which all of a sudden seemed so bloody appealing.

Apparently I was already in the fourth stage of grief, which Wikipedia uses quotations such as *"I'm so sad, why bother with anything?"* and *"I'm going to die soon so what's the point?"* to help explain. I don't know about you, but that sounds just like how I felt before I'd met my dad anyway, and I don't remember experiencing the first three stages at any point, so from where I'm standing, Kübler-Ross's depression model is pretty damn poor.

Her final stage, "acceptance", might be

right though, because around a year after the Hubba Bubba bubble burst (try saying that in a rush), I had finally started to get over myself and was thinking about the future. I didn't know *exactly* what I wanted to do for the rest of my time as part of a society far from the brink of termination, but I had decided to study psychology at Edge Hill University, which if nothing else, sounds upper class enough to perhaps get you laid every once in a while with someone who doesn't know what 280 UCAS points equates to. I'm about to back this claim up with a very important anecdote, which marks the first chapter in the rest of my life.

Believe it or not, I was at a zombie pub crawl. Nice to know that university had matured me, right? There must have been nearly a hundred of us walking through the streets of Manchester at 10 o'clock wearing face paint and ripped clothes, and the reactions of the civilians (yes, I really will distance myself by using that term) was quite something to behold. We'd all met online so didn't really know each other, but it didn't matter. After pub number eight, we'd drunk so much that we didn't really need to put on a zombie-walk anymore.

A fellow zombie, Christie, bought me a drink somewhere between pub eleven and fifteen. She seemed pretty attractive and I figured if she looked alright with fake blood all over her chin, she had to look good with no clothes on, so before I could even use one of the six zombie chat up lines I had pre-prepared, I'd identified myself as an Edge Hill student and asked her if she wanted to come back to my flat. Clearly my charm is as irresistible as the rumours say – we exited the pub via a taxi, and a slightly bemused driver, to my student accommodation.

Once we got in, there wasn't a lot of hanging around. Truth be told, she didn't look as good in the buff as I'd expected, and I even considered offering her some more face paint so she could do up the rest of her body to match her visage, but I figured she might think I had some kind of weird zombie fetish.

To spare you the gory details for a change, let's skip forward to Chapter Two of my life. I like to call it *The Phone Call Trilogy*, and it's set three weeks later:

"Andy? It's Christie."

"Christie! I'm so glad you called! I've been thinking about you all week and that fantastic night that we sha–" (I was going to say "shared" before I was interrupted by the way – mind out of the gutter.)

"Andy, I'm pregnant."

ZOMG.

And so, another twist in the tale. Before I had chance to work out how I felt about this unexpected revelation, she threw in a second curveball:

"And I'm going to get rid of it. I just thought you ought to know."

And so, once again I was faced with the issue of not knowing exactly what I would have done in a life changing situation – would *I* have wanted to keep the baby? Would I have lived with Christie, or had it at weekends? I would never know, because that choice had been taken away from me before I'd even had the chance to make it.

Only this time, I was surprisingly much more positive. My desire to become a father had been fluctuating ever since I had first thought about it, the knowledge of how much of a scumbag I might have been preventing me from fully comprehending that I could still play happy families. But now that there was a physical combination of my DNA with that of another sad zombie fanatic growing contentedly in a biological oven, this future suddenly seemed so much more plausible. So what if she didn't want to keep the baby? That was a minor setback. I'd soon talk her round. Making the most of this rare optimistic mindset I had found myself in, I called her back:

"Christie? It's Andy."

"I know – I've saved your number."

"...Right. Listen, I think we should keep the baby."

"Oh really? And where did this epiphany come from?"

"I just think... like... it might be a laugh."

I didn't mean that. *You* know I didn't mean that and *I* know I didn't mean that. But she didn't. I just couldn't think of what to say. I knew how much of a light-hearted, fun-loving person she had seemed the night of the pub crawl and thought I might be able to play to that side of her. Of course, *most* people are light-hearted and fun loving after 13 WKDs and 8 Vodka shots, so perhaps the real Christie was more serious than I had first expected.

"A laugh."

"What I mean is: I think it could be what we both need. A baby might... give us a sense of purpose in life. It might be what we were meant to do."

"Don't get all philosophical on me, Andy. You don't know the slightest thing about me other than I go to zombie pub crawls and I have a picture of Jimmy Hendrix taking a dog for a walk tattooed on my hip."

"I still think it looked more like a pig..."

"You probably don't even know my surname!"

"Well... that's not completely relevant, considering he'd take my name anyway..."

"Oh, so you're assuming our baby is a boy now?"

"Well it's not going to be *anything* if you kill it, is it!?"

Even *I* could hear the pain in my voice in that last one. That'd definitely do the trick.

"Andy, look, I couldn't possibly have this baby even if I wanted it. I'm starting the second year of my degree soon and I have a boyfriend. He'd kill me."

Now, I'm no Inspector Morse, but something didn't add up here. She had a boyfriend. Then–

"How do you know it's mine?"

"What?"

"If you have a boyfriend, how do you know this thing's mine?"

"My boyfriend's in Afghanistan."

"Oh."

"He's not been home for four months."

"Ah."

"So… yeah."

The awkward silence that followed allowed me to think a few things through. So, I was nothing more than a plot device in a drunken, one night stand. Ok, I knew that anyway. But now there was an even slimmer chance of Christie keeping my child. In fact, there was probably more chance of the epidemic.

But it didn't matter. I still wanted my baby. If anything, I would fight even harder to keep him alive now that I knew fighting was my only option.

But I had no game plan. I tried to come up with one after the sequel, but all I could think about was how much he needed to be alive. How this was my only chance at making a difference to the world: succeeding where my father had failed. My motivation for being a dad grew stronger every day, but for the life of me, I didn't know what to do next. And time was running out.

Two days later, the third phone call:

"Andy? It's... it's Christie."

"I know – I've saved your number." OK, I probably shouldn't have tried to be smart considering how upset she sounded.

"Can... can you come over?"

Welcome back to the stage my long lost friend: Mr Indecision. The last time I had been with Christie, she had used me for sex, resulting in a pregnancy which if she had not already, would soon be attempting to abort. However, there must have been a reason she wanted me with her, and if there were, there was a chance that she would want to keep my baby, right?

Right. Just trust me on this.

So I went round. Her face was prettier than I remembered it from under the face paint but there were large red rings around her eyes – she had been crying. A lot.

"It's... it's Mark," she said, apparently struggling not to burst into tears again.

"Who's Mark?"

"My... my boyfriend."

"Oh you mean the guy you cheated on with m–"

"He's dead!"

Awkward.

And then the sobbing erupted. I took her over to the couch where she cried continuously into my *'Zombie Response Unit'* T-shirt for over an hour. Eventually, she told me about how he had been killed in an explosion while escorting a team to recover some IED components. Since then I've found IED to stand for Improvised Explosive Devices, but it doesn't add much to the story – at the end of the day, he died whilst she was at home making love to someone she'd only known a few hours, and I could tell she was feeling pretty guilty. Understandably.

I had sensed an opportunity however. After making her a strong cup of coffee in her refreshingly organised kitchen, I sat her down and told her what I had been through when my dad died, and how it would eventually get easier. All leading up to:

"So, have you thought about what you're going to do with the baby?"

"Wha... what do you mean?" she sniffed.

"Well, now that your boyfriend's snuffed it, there's nothing stopping you from squeezing my sprog out for me," I thought.

"I know it's a very hard time, but you don't want to do anything rash," I said.

"Like what?"

"Like aborting a baby you might later decide would have been best to keep. Would Mark really want someone *else* to die?"

"Er... *yes*? Because it wasn't *his*?"

"At the end of the day, without sounding harsh, you're never going to be able to have that future with him now, as much as you might have liked to. You need to start looking at what other options you have."

"Like having a baby with *you*?"

The stress on the word "you" like I was some sort of demonic flesh addict was slightly insulting, but I plodded on:

"Yes. Like having a baby with me."

"Andy, what are my family going to think if I tell them that my boyfriend's died *and* that I'm pregnant with someone else's child, all on the same day!?"

"You could tell them about the pregnancy another day if that makes it any easier..."

"Andy, this is not what I want. I can't have a baby with you! I met you last month at a zombie pub crawl! I hardly know you!"

"You've got nine months to get to know me! Trust me, I'm not that bad!"

"I don't care if you're the male epitome of Mother Theresa! I–"

"Just so you know, there are some historians that actually think she was a bit of a bitch..."

"Andy, I don't want a baby. I don't care whose it is. That's not something I want to do with my life yet. I'm only young."

"Then let *me* have it. Have the baby and let me keep it. You'll never hear from us again if you don't want to. Please. This is what I need to do with my life. This is what I *have* to do."

"Andy, it's not just about you! It's not you that's got to carry the thing around for nine months."

"But it's not just about *you* either Christie... you're not thinking of the cultural implications!"

"I'm sorry?"

"I don't know if you remember, but when our little boy–"

"Or girl."

"–Or girl," I added quickly, remembering who was in the driving seat at this moment in time, "when our... *child* was being... made, the two of us looked remarkably like zombies. Correct me if I'm wrong, but surely you must be curious as to whether this could be an influencing factor in the birth of the first zombie baby on our planet? You owe it to your country to have this child, whether you like it or not!"

Before she could stop herself, she was laughing. There were tears of sadness on her face and a baby of indeterminate life in her belly, but I had made her chuckle with the (slightly) witty trump card I had brought into her flat before I'd even known her boyfriend was dead.

"Promise me you'll think about it?" I asked her in a serious tone when she'd finally stopped laughing.

She paused.

"OK," she said finally. "I promise."

Now I know from experience that when women promise something, it's considerably more genuine than when men do, so I was filled with a sense of optimism when I left her flat after a slightly awkward hug. I only really acknowledged its awkwardness a day later when she hadn't rang. But my memory of it became more and more awkward as the week went on, and when we hit the one week mark, my optimism had packed its suitcase and done a runner, and I was left with a nagging worry.

I was determined not to pester her – she needed space to make up her own mind – but I had four variations on a "you'd better not have aborted our baby" theme in my text message drafts at the ready. I was getting worried...

And then, halfway through level 42 of Nazi Zombies (yes, I am *that* good), another phone call, milking a classic trilogy, Indiana Jones style:

"Hi Andy, it's Christie."

"Hi. Wh... how are you?"

"I'm fine. Look, I've been thinking about what you said. About us keeping the baby. I could see how much it means to you, and... well I think it's quite touching that you *want* to be a dad so much. That's really rare these days."

Oh, hi Optimism! You're back!

"And I like you. I think you're funny, and... nice." Hmm, empty adjective... "But, I just don't know you well enough to make such a massive commitment."

Oh, bye then.

"But you've liked everything you've seen so far Christie! Please, you've got to g–"

"Please let me fini–"

"Bu–"

"Let. Me. Finish.

"I don't know you well enough to say I'm going to start a family with you. I've met you twice in my life. Which is why I'm willing to say: yes, I'll have the baby and we can try and get to know each other over the next eight months. If it doesn't work out, you can have it, under the condition that you provide the money to make the rest of my year at uni still achievable. And when I can't get to lectures, you go for me and you get everything I need."

In my head, that didn't really sound like such a great plan. If she wasn't going to the university herself, I couldn't see her being very successful with her studies. However, I thought now was probably not the best time to voice this opinion, and of course I had no objection if it guaranteed me a shot at Dad. Screw *my* degree – what good's psychology to anyone anyway?

And so it began.

Things were weird at first. The first date somehow isn't quite as exciting when you know she's already pregnant. The trepidation of trying to decide whether holding her hand in the cinema will create too much sweat to put her off you is lost when you've already done the deed that you usually build towards through several dates. (Or half a pack of Rolos if you live where I do.) We had skipped the tentative stage. We needed to genuinely find out if we could and should spend the rest of our lives with each other, and time was growing short. There was so much riding on this whole ordeal it was untrue, so that any light-hearted happiness had the constantly looming decision-time hanging over it: would the family be two or three?

What I really wanted was my kid, and I was getting him (ok, or her) now either way. But the more time I spent with Christie, and the more the possibility of the three of us starting a family sprung to life in my head, the less I could imagine anything else. Who wants to raise a kid by themselves? It had been hell for my mum. Could I really go through all that again but through the other pair of eyes? I didn't know.

Generally, I'd say things were going ok. We probably went out twice a week and I stayed at hers another two or three nights. I cooked for her. I'd barely even cooked for myself before. Admittedly, I was making crap at first, but it was something we could laugh about together. Two weeks, three cook books and a bit of googling later, and we were eating proper meals, cooked by my fair hands. She did it a few times too, but I made a point of doing it more than she did. I wanted her to see that if we did decide to stay together, she wouldn't have to worry about being a housewife for the rest of her life. I'm great at deluding people like that.

But we were getting on. We both liked *Shaun of the Dead* more than *Zombieland*. We shared a panic when the Wii Fit told us how disastrous our posture was. We both even had the same number of Facebook friends, proof if there ever was any that one of us wasn't beneath the other. Ok, so she had a *few* more than me, but it'd be really weird if she had *exactly* the same...

I mean don't get me wrong, there was the odd awkward moment. But that was understandable – it wasn't a normal situation. We were under a lot of pressure. Most of the time though, things were as good as could be expected. Even meeting the parents wasn't *that* bad, all things considered, and our friends were all pretty understanding. Or hers were anyway; I know that a lot of mine thought I was crazy, because to them, women are good for sex, cooking and someone to explain the offside rule to so they feel clever. I don't know how they ever hope to start a family with that outlook, but I didn't care: they were wrong. Christie was great. She filled a hole in my life that I didn't even know was there and it didn't matter what anyone else thought – this was about us three and no one else.

But then things started to take a turn for the worse. I don't know what was going wrong – to be honest I thought we'd been getting on great – but the fatter she got, it seemed the grumpier she got too. I did my best to keep things fun, but the more I tried, the more I felt she was getting bored with me, and one step closer to making the decision I desperately hoped she wouldn't. I kept telling myself it was the hormones, but I'd never heard it being this bad: One night she was crying over Mark. The next she was in a "private" phone call with her friend (that was made impossible for me not to hear) about what a mess she'd made of her life, what her parents thought of her and how much she was ****ing up her degree. The next she ended it.

"You can't do this. It was going so well at the start. It–"

"At the *start*, Andy – not anymore!"

"You're just hormonal – it's normal!"

"I might be hormonal, but I'm not delusional! It's never going to work out Andy, we're just too different!"

"How are we too different?? We're both zombie fanatics! You're probably the most un-different person to me that exists!"

"That's where it starts and ends, Andy, I'm sorry–"

"We're going to have a baby!"

"So we should get *married*? Because we shared a drunken night after a bar crawl when I was at my most fertile time of the month and my boyfriend wasn't around? It's not a basis for happiness Andy, you have to see that."

I didn't. I didn't see it. How could two people who'd created the miracle of a human embryo not be able to have a decent future together? It didn't make any sense.

So yeah, I was upset. But it *was* her decision. Other than lock her in a room and perform a home birth (which I swear had barely crossed my mind), I couldn't force her into staying with me, and verbal manipulation would only go so far.

My main worry though was for my baby. I should have made Christie sign some kind of contract to guarantee that either way, he/she/it

51

was mine. But when I brought this up, she assured me she was still intent on keeping her initial promise. Things could still go according to plan (B).

And they did. Right until my beautiful baby girl (ok, so my psychic powers aren't up to scratch) was born. I was there of course. Not holding Christie's leg in the air or anything, but sitting quietly at the side, anxious to meet my child, clutching the Entonox tube at the ready – that stuff was great for my nerves.

"She's... so beautiful," Christie said, cradling our child.

"Can I hold her?" I asked. It had been at least ten minutes now.

"W... yes," Christie said, handing her over to me a little hesitantly.

She was the most beautiful thing I have ever laid eyes on. Ok, so she looked like she'd just narrowly escaped a horde of the walking dead, but I didn't care. This was the first time my offspring was breathing air into her lungs – I was going to savour it.

"Hello you," I said to her, feeling tears well in my eyes for the first time that night if we're excluding when Christie was clenching her fingers together through my arm. "Shhhhhhh," I said to try and stop the baby's crying. "It's all over now." I was already doing the baby voice without even thinking about it – I was a natural. "You're here, with me, in our world. I'm... I'm your daddy, and I'm going to take care of you now. Yes I am. Yes I *am*!"

"Er, Andy, about that..." Christie said, looking down at the blankets that were covering her so as to avoid my eyes.

"What?"

"...Maybe this isn't the best time."

"*What?*" I had tried to keep my voice as un-heated as possible, but I saw a reflection of the nurse turning round behind me to check everything was ok as I raised my decibels.

"Andy, there's no way I'm going to be able to give her away. I didn't think I'd get this attached, but I'm already... maternal or whatever they call it. I can see why you were so desperate to have a child now. She's my daughter. How could I give her away after carrying her round with me for the best part of a year?"

I was stunned. This couldn't be happening. She couldn't just go back on our agreement like this. It wasn't fair. We had a deal...

"But I won't be unfair. I'm sure the courts will be able to sort something out so you can have her every couple of weekends or..."

She trailed off, but I wasn't listening. This wasn't right. It had been *me* that had wanted the baby. *Christie* had wanted to get rid of it. I'd convinced her into giving it, and us, a chance, but she'd discarded both of those ideas. Now, she wanted the kid for herself and nothing to do with me! And of course, the law would side with her because she was the mother. Is it fair that because someone is born with ovaries, they automatically have more rights to a child's upbringing? I'd have been the one to carry her around for nine months had it been biologically possible.

I looked down at her in my arms. She was the first real opportunity I'd ever had to make something of myself. I *was* going to be a dad. I was going to be a bloody good one. As I concreted that in my mind, the door of the maternity ward grew into focus at the edge of my vision. I knew that I may never get this opportunity again...

And I was gone. Clutching my daughter as if she was the only copy of the cure for cancer, I burst through the doors and into the main hallway. I looked left and right – which way had I come in? I began sprinting in the direction of my answer, heads turning as I ran.

Then the shouting started. I turned and saw three nurses who had been at the birth behind me, chasing me down the corridor. (Two of them were men by the way, but don't worry, I'd have made the same assumption.) Christie was with them too, looking embarrassingly similar to how she had during in the pub crawl.

I turned a corner so they were out of my line of sight, only to run into a lifeless member of staff pushing a trolley. She looked at the screaming baby in my hands, bewildered but I pushed her to one side and hurtled down the corridor. As we reached the bottom, I looked back and saw that she had recovered and was holding something black with an aerial to her ear – reinforcements would be on the way soon.

As we neared the exit of the building and

the freedom which preceded it, a host of zombies wearing black appeared from God knows where, blocking my path. Her walkie-talkie had worked. They began sprinting towards me, so I turned back, only to find what could have been their reflection in a mirror from the other side. We were trapped.

I dived through a door on my left and found myself in a short little corridor and then a ward full of patients. Some were screaming and so was my daughter. I was beginning to think I should have considered the "stealth mode" option...

I got to the end of the ward. A dead end? I looked through the window and saw we were on the first floor. (Or is it the second floor? It always confuses me. The one above the bottom floor is the one we were on.) Although I think I could have survived a jump from that height, I wasn't so keen on doing it with my twenty-minute-old baby in my arms. As I looked out of the window though, I saw an ambulance pull up under it, the driver speaking to someone on the pavement. There was a God.

Another one of those moments where I

wished someone was recording my life... In the corner of my eye the army of darkness was heading towards us, inaudible shouting threatening to consume us from all angles. I jumped onto the bed next to me, apologising quickly to the woman who lay in it (always one to maintain manners even in intense situations) and flung myself sideways through the glass window, shielding my prize with both arms. The impact on my shoulder was hard, but I hadn't been expecting cling film. I kept my head down to completely shield her, and amazingly, no glass lodged itself in us.

We landed exactly where I had intended – on the roof of the ambulance which had nearly halved the distance we'd had to fall. Ok, so I lost my footing when I landed and fell on my back, but I had stayed on the roof, and my baby was fine. Chuck Norris would be proud.

Bounding off the bonnet, I flew into the huge car park, hoping my weaving between cars would confuse anybody who might be following the route I was taking. Finally, I reached Tommy's car that he had let me drive there in (he's not just my friend so I can get to places, I swear), opened it up and sped out of the car park with my daughter on my lap.

Driving away from the hospital, I began to try to put things in perspective. What should I do now? Where could I go?

And all of a sudden, I had finally come up with a conclusion to the internal dilemma I'd been dwelling on for years. Having my world ripped savagely apart from all around me by the mindless armies of a compassionless society, I was forced to finally decide what I would do if there was a zombie epidemic. The simple solution I'd seen countless times in TV programmes, films, comic books and the like now made perfect sense to me:

I'd find us somewhere to hide. We'd live together in our shelter, protected from those that would cause us harm. Every additional second spent together would be cherished – father and daughter, together against the world.

I'll hold on for as long as humanly possible.

Bubbles

"Coz you're all friends of mine…" Michael sang.

They weren't. He knew four people in the audience. It's not that he wouldn't *like* to meet the thousands who had bought his records and had now turned up to see him perform in Manchester, England. He would have loved to meet them individually, see what his music meant to them, but it was just physically impossible. He wouldn't know where to start.

"And when my life is over, I'll remember when we were together…" he continued, without his microphone. He usually performed the end of the final song without the assistance of a microphone and with little backing. He had always said that the tour would rely primarily on his vocals rather than the creation of a huge spectacle, and this was a good way to demonstrate that, whilst hopefully being a satisfying conclusion to the performance.

He raised his hands to stop a few screams

before the final line. There were usually at least two drunken girls near the stage who decided to make themselves heard whilst he tried to project to a whole arena. Those were people he did *not* want to meet.

"Coz we were alone...and I was singing my song for you."

The end.

The crowd went wild, most of them having not expected the discarding of the microphone. There were arms clapping in the air, cheering, and screaming which was now appropriate. Michael took a few seconds to absorb this – nothing was more satisfying than the appreciation of thousands of people after a well-performed gig. This was why he was still doing it.

Never one to milk the final applause too much, he gestured a thanks to the band and the crowd themselves and walked off the stage. Verbal congratulations surrounded him backstage, but this meant little – he didn't need to impress his friends. His tour manager said a few words to him too, but he wasn't really listening – he needed to go and get his phone and ring Lu like he promised he would after the show.

He started to make his way to the container where his things (and phone) would be, but was interrupted when someone grabbed him urgently by the shoulders.

"Quick – come with me!"

He was rushed quickly down some steps as there was shouting from above.

"What?" he asked the two men who had taken him down there. "What's wrong?"

"Security breach," one of them said, breathing heavily as he ran. "We just need to get you out of here as quickly as possible."

Michael didn't ask any other questions as he was rushed through the complex web of corridors which he hadn't known existed. As he ran he could still hear shouting from somewhere, but it was not close.

"There's a huge black limo speeding off as we speak," one of the security guys told him. "So people think you're in it. You'll be leaving through a different exit in a much less conspicuous vehicle momentarily."

Michael was familiar with this procedure. It

was one that they had practiced many times after high profile gigs in certain countries. What he was not familiar with however was the security team texting on the job. He couldn't help but bring this to their attention as they ran.

"Letting us know the car will be here in one minute," the man replied. Michael couldn't help but feel this was all very unprepared and amateur.

Soon, they stopped at a side door with a fire exit sign above. It did not look like an exit designed for an award-winning singer, security breach or no security breach.

"Here," one of the men panted, pulling a red piece of fabric from his pocket and handing it to him. "Put this on."

Michael unfolded the garment.

"A Spider-Man mask?"

"That's the best we have I'm afraid. It's in case anyone we don't want to see you recognizes you."

"Who?" he asked, pulling the mask over his head.

"We don't know," the man said, taking Michael's suit jacket off him as a waiter would –

presumably that was too much of a giveaway as to who he was as well. "But it's under control. We just need you out of the way."

The phone rang and was answered instantly.

"Ok," the man said, before putting it down. "She's here."

They opened the door and walked on either side of him to the vehicle: a black cab. Michael couldn't help but find this slightly amusing – only in Britain would this be his escape vehicle.

One of the men opened the door for him and he sat in the middle of the seat at the back of the vehicle. On the single seat opposite sat a middle aged woman in a grey pinstripe suit. Her serious expression and Bluetooth earpiece instantly relaxed him somewhat – she looked prepared.

The security guard who opened the door for Michael followed him in and sat on that side of him, and the other one got in the other side. As soon as the doors were closed, the cab pulled away from the sidewalk and set off.

"I've never made a high speed getaway in a cab before," he said, trying to make light of the situation. No response. "So what's the plan then?"

The woman looked at him for a second as if trying to decide what to tell him before she spoke.

"You know what, I'm just going to be upfront with you. This is embarrassing enough as it is without lying about it too. The truth is... we're kidnapping you."

After he had processed what she had just said, he looked either side of him at the men's expressions. They stared sternly in front of them, and one had his hand resting in his inside jacket pocket.

"Guns I presume?" Michael asked, indicating his observation.

The woman nodded. Michael felt sweat start to creep across his forehead, and did not put it down to the mask he was wearing.

"Purely precautionary I assure you. In case you try to escape or start shouting. But I know you're not that stupid Michael."

He looked to the sides again and through the windows. It was dark, they were moving quickly and he was in a foreign country –

attempting to remember the way they were going was fruitless.

"So what do you want with me? I presume you're holding me to ransom?"

"Er... no actually. I... I want you to sing for me."

Ok, so that was unexpected.

"Well it's a marvellous night for a–" he started.

"Very funny," she interrupted, clearly not impressed by his attempt at humour. "Let's hope *tomorrow* night is as marvellous, because *that*'s when you'll be singing."

"What's the occasion?" he asked.

She took a deep breath before beginning. "I work for one of, (if not *the*) largest banks in the world. I'm at the top end of the company, but unfortunately, the recession means they still have to make cuts. Basically I either get promoted, or lose my job entirely. The new job would involve me being able to put on a good dinner party, so..."

"So you want me to provide the entertainment," he finished for her.

"Precisely."

She was deluded. Deranged. It would be all over the news by tomorrow that he was missing, and even if it wasn't, it would be soon afterwards – her employers would know what she had done before the week was up. "And you'll let me go afterwards?"

She nodded.

"How do I know?"

"Well…" she said patronisingly, as if he was being stupid. "After the dinner party, if it became public knowledge that you were missing, everyone at the bank would know that I had kidnapped you. So I'm going to *have* to give you back."

But they'll know anyway, Michael thought. *This won't be kept a secret*. He decided not to voice this obvious flaw in her plan.

"Go on, you can say it," she prompted him.

"What?"

"You're wondering how this won't become public knowledge anyway, but you don't want to say in case I decide to kill you now."

Ok, so she *had* thought of something.

"We left your team an anonymous message telling them that we have you, but will give you back if they don't say anything. They won't call the police because... I know things about them that they don't want getting out."

She couldn't have seen him raise his eyebrows under the mask, but answered his unvoiced question anyway:

"I work at the high end of a bank, Michael. I know stuff. I speak to people who know stuff. It was very easy for me to highlight to your record company a few... blemishes in their tax procedures over the last several years. Blemishes that, if discovered, would mean they could never produce another digital download, let alone a large scale money-making tour like the one I've just interrupted."

She seemed to be enjoying explaining her master plan, letting him know how powerless he was.

"The message said exactly what will happen," she continued. "If you sing for me tomorrow, I'll let you go afterwards and the media will be blissfully unaware of the disappearance of one of its favourite stars *and* hundreds of thousands of pounds of unpaid tax. You'll even be back in time for your next gig –

Birmingham isn't it?"

Michael didn't know what to say – could this be true? He'd always thought Reprise Records had been completely legitimate, but they weren't exactly going to brag about any discrepancies to *him* were they?

"So?" she asked, after half a minute's silence. "What do you say? Will you sing for us?"

"...It's not like I've got much choice is it?"

"Of course you do. But you're not stupid. You should be able to tell by now that I mean business, and that if you don't sing for me when I've gone to all this trouble, there will be serious consequences."

He didn't ask what those would be. He had already decided that he would do it – it was only singing after all. This is what he did for a living and after tomorrow he could go back to his life. Back to the tour. Back to Lu.

If they let him go.

He sat in silence for the rest of the journey. The woman did not ask him any more questions and instead only spoke to the two "security" guys, but about nothing of significance. After about half an hour, she pulled the mask from his head.

"That's the best looking Spider-Man *I've* ever seen," she said. "You really are just as handsome in the flesh."

Ignoring her, he looked out of the window and saw why she had taken the mask off – they had arrived. The car passed through a huge set of gates which opened when the driver put a code into a keypad through the window, driving into a huge set of grounds that dwarfed Michael's own.

A tall hedge framed the property which, illuminated by old-fashioned street lamps, consisted of a huge expanse of neatly cut grass dotted with several large trees and a river which ran parallel to the long track they were now driving along.

"So *how* desperate is this promotion...?" he asked ironically.

"Do not let this deceive you," she told him. "Like most people, I am not without debts."

At the end of the enormous track was a house that the word "mansion" did not do justice to. It looked like several houses had been joined neatly together, with three storeys and several outbuildings, all under beautiful thatched roofing. The river disappeared through a small gap in the wall, seeming to enter the house itself.

"So," Michael said, taking in size of the house which was beyond anything even he was used to, "is there a *Mr* crackpot to join you in your castle, or is it just you?"

"Thinking of the sleeping arrangements already, are you Michael?" He said nothing. "Don't worry, my husband left months ago."

Well that was a surprise.

The car entered the garage and he was walked through the house, which was as beautifully furnished as the grounds were well kept. Eventually, they got to an ensuite bedroom with a double bed.

"This is where you will be staying," she told him. "Is there anything you need before I leave you?"

"You don't have one of those machines that cuts through windows do you?"

"The boys will be outside your room all night," she said, indicating to the security guards who had been with them for the entirety of the journey. "But if you need any more company, I made sure I gave you a particularly roomy bed…"

"I think I'll be alright," Michael said, giving her a fake smile. "I'll see you tomorrow."

"You will indeed," she said. "Get some sleep, tomorrow might be the smallest audience on your tour, but it's your most important one."

*

"Are you going to eat that or just push it round your plate?"

The latter. He felt sick. He wouldn't be able to eat until he knew he was safe.

"I don't eat much," he lied.

"Ok, fine," the woman said. "Follow me. I'll show you where you'll be performing."

He stood up and followed her through the house, escorted by one of her excessively muscly minions that had accompanied them on the journey there the day before. They reached a large room which was unlike anything he had ever seen before. It was made of old mahogany and had large glass doors on one wall which led outside onto some decking. There was a traditional-looking bar at one end of the room that you would expect to see in a hotel. At the other end was what could only be described as a waterfall, pouring slowly from a hole in the wall and disappearing again into the floor. In the middle of the room was where the water no doubt ended up, and the room's most stunning feature: a large Jacuzzi which could have accommodated about twenty people, sunk into the floor and bubbling gently.

"That's usually meant for drinks," she said, pointing at a square platform in the middle of it. "But that's where you'll be singing."

"I'm sorry?"

"You heard."

"And what, all these people you're trying to impress are going to be *in* the pool?"

"Perhaps."

"Are you sure this is appropriate for a dinner party with your superiors…?"

"Michael, don't try and tell me what's appropriate and what's not. These people spend the majority of their time stuck behind desks looking at endless numbers on screens and pieces of paper – they're always glad of something new and exciting… Half of them are in the Mile High Club! They want to know that I can join in with their extravert social-scene, give them something different to brag to their friends about. What could be more exciting than drinking champagne in a Jacuzzi whilst having a private show by Michael Bu–"

"Fine. Whatever. I can't exactly argue with you can I?"

"Not if you want me to let you go, no."

"So do I have a band…?"

She laughed. "I'm afraid not. But I did go to the trouble of downloading the backings on Pirate Bay. The same songs and the same order you've been doing on your tour. There are hidden speakers around the room and someone will be making sure the next song comes on at the right time."

"Classy," he said.

"Mock me all you want," she spat, and he could see real madness in her expression for the first time, seemingly from nowhere. "You're going to sing for me tonight so that I get the promotion I deserve, and you're going to enjoy it. You're going to stand on that square and perform your little heart out and afterwards, you're going to make small talk to the bankers and their wives until they're bored of you, which let's face it, probably won't be too long.

"I have armed guards around my entire property in case you try to escape. You know just by the fact that I was able to kidnap you in the first place that I have sufficient manpower, so don't even *consider* that I am bluffing. You *will* be killed. An arrangement will be struck with your record company to tell the press that you left the country in the middle of your tour and went into a stress-induced early retirement."

She wasn't lying. Michael could tell that this was a previously established contingency plan and that she meant every word.

The man who had escorted them here handed Michael some folded clothes on her command.

"Here's your suit. Put it on. Don't worry, we know it fits."

"Now?"

"Yes. My guests will be here within the hour. You will be stood waiting for us and start singing as we arrive."

He started to get changed in front of them. Nakedness was the least of his worries now. Getting into a suit by himself however was something he was no longer used to.

"*Ooof!* No wonder you don't do any Robbie-Williams-style striptease videos. And you say you don't each much..." He ignored her and continued dressing himself.

"Do you need to use the toilet?" she asked when he was done.

"No."

"Then get him up there Ian."

The bodyguard whose name he had only just found out took his own trousers and shoes off. He then picked Michael up by the legs and swung him over his shoulder. Ok, so all that muscle wasn't just for show. He carefully stepped into the hot tub and walked through the water until they got to the platform, on which he placed Michael, who had not gotten wet at all. He was handed a microphone.

"Prepare yourself," the woman said to him before turning on her heel.

Four men entered the room as she and Ian

left. They seemed unarmed and stood silently in each corner, holding circular trays of nibbles that they had brought in. Michael knew though that should he try to escape, they'd be on him in a flash. He could do nothing now but wait to perform.

He sat down on the platform, stared at the bubbling water around him and started to really think through his predicament. Understandably, he was worried, but he had felt incredibly sick all day, as if there was something more his subconscious was telling him he should be worried about. He started to think it through:

What was going to happen after the party? Was she going to let him go?

Surely she knew that he would go straight to the authorities about what had happened, even if it meant the end of his contract with Reprise Records. Someone else would sign him. She *must* know that he wasn't going to let her get away with this?

She must know.

Suddenly, realisation started to sink in. Of course she knew. She wasn't going to let him just walk free so that he could tell people what had happened. *"You will be killed. An arrangement will be struck with your record company to tell the press that you left the country in the middle of your tour and went into a stress-induced early retirement."*

Maybe that had been her plan all along. Maybe she was going to kill him tonight no matter what happened.

Yes. That made more sense. No one would ever know about what she had done if he was out of the picture. Reprise would keep quiet because of their debts... If that story was even true. If that wasn't just another lie to make him believe he was going to be set free.

It was making his head hurt. He just knew that if he *was* set free, he would make sure that she was arrested. And that unless she really was insane, she would know that too. She was not going to let that happen.

He was going to die. He was going to be murdered as soon as the guests had left.

He needed to escape. He needed to think of a way out, now. Before they arrived. Or he'd be dead by midnight.

The more he tried to come up with *some*

kind of plan, the harder it was to be productive. Time seemed to perpetuate as the brutal reality of his situation sunk in. The sickness in his stomach had escalated from "bad hangover" to something else entirely. He could hardly move, was going to vomit any second and had started to shake. He felt like he was going to die.

He *was* going to die.

Suddenly there was music playing from all around him. He had heard the brass crescendo opening of the song he started his gigs with hundreds of times, but for the first time it sounded truly menacing.

The doors opened and a group of people started to enter the room.

"My friends..." a familiar voice through a microphone over the top of the music. Welcome to the spa room. Feel free to get in our Jacuzzi, which contains beautiful distilled water from the river on the grounds. How appropriate then that our entertainer's first song is *Cry Me A River*. Ladies and gentlemen, let me introduce to you the one and only..."

Michael blanked her out. He should be listening to the instrumental. He needed to know when to come in…

"Now you say you're lonely…" he began. "You cried the whole night through… well you can cry me a river… cry me a river… I cried a river over you."

The brass instrumental was back. He had made it this far without throwing up. He took the opportunity to look at the people who had entered the room: a lot of older men wearing suits who, despite being faced with Canada's biggest star, did not look impressed by the tacky introduction to the night's entertainment. Michael knew straight away that even if the Mile High Club *had* existed, these men were not members and would not be getting wet tonight.

"And now you say you're sorry, for being so untrue… well you can cry me a river… cry me a river… I cried a river over you."

The men were not alone. Accompanying them were their partners, most of whom were younger and notably more attractive; these were affluent men. Michael saw some of the girls' eyes light up instantly when they saw him, and one screamed.

He continued the song but could feel his

voice begin to shake as she watched him – he had to put on a good show so she couldn't say he had not tried.

"Cry me… a river!" He raised both his arms on the last line as he did in some of the shows.

The women, who had gathered around the sides of the Jacuzzi, let out a round of applause. Michael saw some of the men clap, but many just looked at each other with stern disapproval. It was obvious she had made a big mistake assuming this extravagancy would be appreciated.

"Thank you very much," he smiled.

It was clear that his captor was starting to realise what he had. Her voice was shakier than *his* had been as she told them again to feel free to get in the Jacuzzi, and that waiters would walk round offering them champagne.

A piano recording began to play.

"All of me, why not take all of me…?" he started the second number, his mind on everything except the delivery. He needed a way out. As soon as the performance was over he could be killed.

He started racking his brain for a plan –

escape routes, who he could trust, where he had the most chance of being captured…

As he tried to think though, he couldn't help but be distracted by a series of events that had started to take place. One of the younger looking women had returned from the bar where most of the men were (presumably they considered the waiters to be superfluous) and was now starting to undress – perhaps she had asked her husband's permission. Michael assumed she would be getting into the Jacuzzi in her underwear, but it seemed she was planning on wearing them again later. Apparently none of them had been told to bring a swimming costume.

"Oh the shark has pretty teeth dear…"

She entered the Jacuzzi.

"And it shows them, pearly white…"

Some of the other girls walked over to the bar too. Some started to undress where they were.

By the end of *Mack The Knife,* there were eight beautiful women sat staring up at him, the bubbles bursting around their naked bodies. If he wasn't already engaged to a supermodel and he didn't have a death sentence looming over his head, he would have been enjoying himself.

A death sentence.

He needed to come up with a solid plan.

Fast.

"You're a falling star, you're the getaway car…" He looked over at the people at the bar – mainly men. Some of them were watching him. Most were talking amongst themselves.

"You're the line in the sand when I go too far…" They didn't know he had been kidnapped. They couldn't – she would never have told them that if she seriously considered getting the job she wanted.

"You're the swimming pool, on an August day…" That was it. He had to use that against her. She would always be nice-as-pie in front of them.

"You're the perfect thing to say." It was a good job he knew these tunes like the back of his hand. He was on autopilot, trying to think of what to do.

Before he could continue his planning, he was distracted again. One of the girls had stood up in the Jacuzzi and was dancing in front of him in all her glory. Some of the others were sitting in what they clearly considered to be provocative positions, so that the bubbles were not quite adequate cover for their modesty. If he wasn't so scared it would be laughable.

By the time he was singing *I've Got The World On A String*, three of the eight girls were leaning on the platform and reaching at his ankles. Had they been drinking before this? Either way, an opportunity had presented itself. And he was not going to let it disappear.

When it hit the recorded sax solo in the middle of the song, he started dancing with the girls, kicking his legs out towards them and allowing them to grab him. When one grabbed his foot, he made to pull away but, as he had hoped, she pulled back. Knowing he had to make this as realistic as he could, he allowed her pulling him to trip him over – off the platform and into the pool.

There were screams. A huge splash. And when he raised his head from the water there was a lot of splashing and laughing from the girls. The microphone floated idly between the bubbles.

Michael looked over to the bar in search for his nameless captor. He found her by one of the greyest of the men and saw her livid expression for a second before it vanished into laughter. Good – she was going to put on a front.

"Oh Michael!" she mock-scolded him over the music, which was now just empty accompaniment.

"The girls were getting too excited!" he shouted, forcing a huge cheeky smile across his face. "They pulled me right in!"

"Ian!" she shouted, and he was to hand in seconds. "Take Michael to dry off and get some new clothes. He can carry on when he's ready!"

He was out of the Jacuzzi, and the wet platform was taken out too. She went over to him and patted him on the back playfully. Everyone was laughing at what had happened. Ian took him out of the room and down a corridor.

"So what's the plan?" he asked. "You got any more clothes that'll fit me?"

"She bought about five sets just in case anything like this happened," Ian said, walking by his side. "Come on."

Now what?

They entered another corridor. As they walked along it Michael noticed the long shelf which lined the edge of the wall. Long thin vases were alternated with picture frames. Knowing this could be his only chance, he picked one up as he walked past, swung it through the air and into Ian's head.

Ian could not get his hands up to protect his face in time and fell to the floor with a large thud. Michael kicked him as hard as he could in the side of the head, hoping that would do it – he had no other ideas.

Ian was still, glass lodged into the side of his head and blood already escaping onto the floor. Michael seemed to think he was still breathing, but he couldn't be sure and didn't have time for a thorough check.

He searched his pockets and found straight away what he was looking for – a mobile phone. He pressed the keypad and the subsequent option for an emergency call (thank God that was there – he couldn't remember the number for the UK) and with the phone to his ear he started to run down the corridor, looking for a place to hide.

"Emergency service?"

But the phone exploded in his hand before he could answer.

Michael looked up and saw a man of a similar build to Ian at the other end of the corridor, pointing a gun at him as the remains of the phone clattered to the floor. It was over.

"WAIT THERE!" the man shouted, and ran towards him, holding the gun.

When he reached where Michael stood, he yelled at him to put his hands behind his head and turn around. He did so, knowing he was defeated, and walked back the way he had come on a prompting nudge from the gun.

As they walked down the corridor, Michael knew this was the end of the line. They approached Ian's body. It was over.

"You..." the man said in horror after seeing where his colleague lay on the floor, illuminated by the chandelier above. "You killed–"

BANG!

Michael raised his arms to protect himself from the shot that had been fired. There was no pain in his body – had he missed?

Then the man's body fell on top of Ian's, blood spurting from the side of his head.

"Come on, this way!"

Another man had appeared from behind, grabbed him by the arm and was running with him down the corridor. They moved off through a bathroom and into another corridor, which they ran down and entered a small room with several chairs and a bookshelf in. The man pulled back on one of the books and the bookshelf started to swivel on a circular platform like a revolving door. They stepped quickly through the gap as it moved and into a cold corridor with no lighting.

"One sec..." the man said, breathing heavily. He pulled out a small torch and sent a thin beam of illumination into the air. "There we are."

"Thank you," Michael said. "You saved me."

"We're not out of the water *just* yet. She will be looking for you when she finds the bodies."

"Why didn't we move them?"

"No time. There were men in the next

corridor along who could have turned the corner any second and seen us. We've just gotta get out of here. Come on, let's go."

He started to walk quickly down the corridor. Michael followed him.

"Who are you?" he asked.

"I'm Carol's butler."

"Carol being–"

"The woman who kidnapped you, yes."

"If you work for her, then why are you–?"

"Because she was going to have you killed after her guests left tonight." He knew it. "I couldn't let that happen... Plus I'm a huge fan of yours."

"...Well that's good to know I guess," Michael said, following the light from the torch ahead of them which was barely illuminating the old wooden walls. "Where exactly are we?"

"We're in a passage which goes through the centre of the mansion. I know for a fact that Carol doesn't know it exists."

"Why not?"

"I came with the house when she bought it. I've been here for years. I knew as soon as I met her there were a few things I should keep to myself."

"How will you get away with helping me escape?"

"I won't, but it won't matter when she's in prison for what she has done."

Michael took a second to run this all over in his head. He felt a huge relief inside him that he had been given a lifeline, but still felt very worried – like he said, they were not safe yet.

"So what's the plan then?"

"We get the **** out of here is what," the man said. "You hear that?"

Michael nodded when he noticed the sound of running water. The man shone his torch ahead and Michael could see a large pool being filled by a waterfall which came from the wall. He remembered how the river had seemingly disappeared into the house when they had arrived, and how Carol had said that the Jacuzzi was filled with distilled water from it.

"What's with the whole water thing you've got going on here?" Michael asked the butler.

"Basically the old owners of the house had the river channelled into it so that they could have an indoor stream through some of the rooms. It was supposed to be relaxing, and it *did* look good to be fair, but it caused more problems than anything else what with dirty water, leaks and the like. Carol decided it was the last straw when she found a dead kitten floating in her bedroom one morning and had the whole thing removed. She had a filtration system put in and now the water's just used to fill up the Jacuzzi. But look at this."

He shone the torch at a white box on the wall. It had a red lever which was pushed near to the bottom, next to the number 5. The numbers went all the way up to 200.

"This was used to control the flow of the water through the house. The more water you let through, the faster it'd move. When she decided to get rid of the stream, I had to put this right down so that it only let in enough water to fill the Jacuzzi. Otherwise it would completely burst the filtration system and destroy her little spa room."

Although Michael could not see the man very well in the dark, he could imagine the fire in his eyes from the excitement in his voice.

"You're not seriously thinking of–?"

"I've waited to do this since she arrived. They're gonna know you've escaped any second anyway, we might as well cause a panic for them, give them something else to worry about while we get out of here."

"Yeah… ok," he said.

"Are you gonna do the honours or am I gonna have to do it?"

The plan did make sense. Michael rammed his hand up on the lever so that it was next to the number 200.

Instantly, things began to change. The noise of the water falling into the pool was no longer a gentle splashing, becoming something you might expect to hear at the bottom of Niagara Falls. The man shone his torch into the pool and they watched as the small hole at the bottom of it, presumably flowing water through a pipe into the filtration system, grew a lot bigger.

"Brilliant," the butler said. "Now let's go before it bursts beneath our feet."

They left the pool, carried on down the corridor, ran up some stairs and took a left turn before the butler told him to stop. He pressed a finger to his lips, crouched down and lifted up one of the floor panels slightly before pulling it back a fraction.

As soon as Michael looked through the small gap he had made, he realised that it was also a ceiling panel for the spa room, which was now below them. He crouched down and could see the girls in the Jacuzzi, looking considerably more bored than when he had last seen them, without the platform in the middle and the entertainment it had supported. The men were still stood at the bar, their expressions even less impressed than they were before, and Carol was in the middle of them, looking anxious and turning her head repeatedly towards the door.

Then the fireworks started. The waterfall at the end of the room grew much quicker and heavier, splashing everywhere. Several large cracks jutted out from the floor at the sides of the Jacuzzi which was right below their vantage point, water spraying quickly out from each one. There was screaming. Then the pipe that was apparently supplying the waterfall burst, and a huge jet of water blasted through the wall, across the room and into the crowd at the bar. Shouting. More screaming. Carol's mouth hung open.

"Come on," the man said, pulling Michael away. "We've got to get out of here."

They ran to the end of the corridor and reached another circular platform which presumably had another bookshelf on the other side.

"We've got to be careful now."

"Why?"

"This is on the main corridor. It's right near the garage, but if anyone sees…"

He trailed off and pushed a button on the wall. The bookshelf started to spin, but as soon as it did, Michael saw one of the guards on the other side who spotted them instantly and reached inside his jacket…

"Shit…" The butler had seen him too.

"RUN!" Michael shouted.

Gunfire broke into their corridor, but they were already pounding back the way they had come, quicker than they'd run yet.

"What's the plan!?" Michael asked as they took a corner.

"We can't go back to the other end. We'd never get through the house without them finding us. There's just one option."

"Where??"

"This is our only way out," the butler said, slowing down and dropping to his knees. "She won't have any guns in there."

The spa room.

"No way!"

"Fine, you stay there then!"

He pulled the panel completely from the floor and jumped through without looking back. Michael looked down and watched him land in the middle of the Jacuzzi which still had two girls in before bobbing his head up. He was fine.

Then more gunfire erupted down the corridor and without another thought, Michael followed him, jumping feet-first through the hole and crashing into the water and onto one of the girls.

"COME ON!" the butler yelled, pulling him from the Jacuzzi before the splash had even finished. Girls were screaming, in and out of the Jacuzzi. People were yelling at them to stop. There was water everywhere.

They ran through the room without stopping to see who was following them and burst out of the glass doors onto the decking, only to meet one of the smaller guards pointing a handgun at them. The butler pushed the gun to the side with one hand and punched the man in the face with the other. He pulled the gun from his hand as he fell to the floor and started to run. Everything was happening so quickly…

The glass shattered behind their heads. Gunfire from somewhere in front of them.

"THIS WAY!"

The shots continued as they ran. Michael's companion held his new weapon out with one hand and fired it across the grass towards the hidden shooters as he moved. Michael could tell they were shooting at them from the far edges of the grounds as he heard the shots miss from what sounded like quite a fair distance behind them.

Then he felt a bullet fly past his ankles. He knew that the longer they were here, the more people would be alerted to his escape and the more chance he had of being killed.

"WHERE ARE WE GOING!?" he yelled.

"IN HERE!" the butler said on cue, as they reached a large outbuilding. They ran round the side and through the door.

Automatic lights came on and illuminated the array of cars inside. Gunfire pounded the walls. The butler picked up some car keys and a small device with an aerial which he threw to Michael. They opened the doors of a yellow sports car and jumped in.

"Do the honours again my friend," the butler said through ragged breath, nodding to what Michael was holding.

He looked down and read the writing next to the only two buttons on the device: *'Garage'* and *'Gate'*. He rammed his finger into *'Garage'* and the metal doors began to tilt open. The butler revved the engine as the bonnet was peppered with bullets.

"GO!" Michael yelled.

They shot out under the door which was only half way open, and began to tear up the track towards the gate, building speed as they went.

"Keep pressing it!" the butler shouted. "As soon as it connects it'll start opening!"

As Michael started repeatedly pushing the *'Gate'* button with his thumb, the window to his left shattered on impact with another bullet. He sunk down in his seat, and heard the thudding against the sides of the car as more shots were fired over the river.

The gates began to open. Michael continued hammering the button anyway.

"Come on..." the butler said under his breath as they flew down the track.

The gap grew wider.

"Come on..."

The bullets continued as they neared the exit.

"COME ON!"

They reached the gate just as it was wide enough to let them through, screeched out onto the road and took off down the lane.

Michael looked out of his now shattered window and saw a huge jet of water over the hedge, spraying into the air like a fountain, most probably through the base of the Jacuzzi and subsequently the house's thatched roof.

"Looks like she won't be getting that promotion after all," he said.

The butler didn't laugh. He continued to tear relentlessly through the lanes before joining the motorway, desperate to get as far away from his old place of work as possible. Michael turned and took his first proper look at the man who had saved his life: He looked to be in his mid-forties, wore a thick black moustache and had a stubbled square jaw which was now clenched in concentration.

Eventually they came off the motorway and pulled up in a layby. They both let out a huge sigh, knowing they had escaped successfully. Michael's body was aching and his head was spinning but it didn't matter; they were alive.

"So what do I call you?" Michael asked, leaning back in his seat.

"Steve," he replied, still panting.

"Steve… you saved my life," Michael said.

"No shit," Steve laughed. He slapped Michael's arm. "Hey, no worries man – you're the king."

He laughed. "If a Michael was the king it was Jackson, not me. But seriously, I can't just say thank you for what you've done for me tonight and leave it at that. I need to go *some* way to pay you back."

Steve laughed.

"I'm serious!"

"Well, we have got three *small* stops to make on the way back. We can call it quits after that."

"Where are we going?"

"I thought, just as a bit of a thank you, we could call in on my wife, my mum and my, er... girlfriend, and you could do them all a bit of a set. Nothing too major, just... I dunno... five or six songs each or something."

"...Are you serious?"

"Well... yeah. Hey, I saved your life remember!"

"Your wife *and* your girlfriend?"

"Yeah, although don't mention that when you get there. Obviously."

"I'll sing for your wife and your mum, but not the girlfriend. It goes against everything I believe in."

As Steve looked at him across the car, Michael could suddenly feel the tension in the air.

"Michael, let me just remind you of the situation you're in. You are stranded in a foreign country, with no money and no phone. There is a crazy woman after you with a host of armed hooligans, desperate to make sure you don't tell the world that she kidnapped you for her little soirée. I have a very fast car and am offering to get you safely to where you need to be if you would just join me on three short pit stops."

"Or I could just get out of the car and ask someone else for a li–"

"And I still have the gun I took from that man."

Michael looked down at the bulge in Steve's jacket pocket and the menacing handle which protruded from it.

He sighed. It was going to be a long night.

Fear's Touch

"Looking up at the sky on a night like this... it's easy to believe that we're not alone – I wonder what's out there..." Becky pondered aloud to her two friends sat either side of her on the park bench.

"Joseph Fear," Josh responded.

Becky sighed. She was sick of this topic – no matter what was being spoken about, it always managed to crop up whenever Josh opened his mouth. Alice beat her to voicing their shared frustration:

"Can you shut *up* about Joseph Fear!? We've been through this. He's not gonna come here."

"But he used to live round here with his mum," Josh regurgitated his favourite argument.

"Here and a dozen other places," Alice was ready to recycle her arguments also. Becky thought this was like watching an episode of Friends she had seen many times before – she

101

knew what was going to be said before the characters did. "Do you really think he'd be stupid enough to come back here when the police are looking for him? He'll be hiding low somewhere."

"But this is near where his mum died! That must mean *something* to him! It's like Harry Potter; he wanted to go to Godric's Hollow to visit his parents'–"

"Did you really just reference Harry Potter? That has literally no relevance in this conversation."

"Course it has. Harry wanted to visit his parents' grave. Fear might too."

"You can't compare a fictional wizard to a real life nutcase." Alice sounded exasperated.

"You can't compare broccoli to a roast potato," Josh said, mimicking a girl's voice from an old TV advert.

"Once again, your grasp of relevance is astounding," Alice said, shaking her head. "What are your predicted A Level grades again...?"

"Don't forget," Becky said, "Joseph Fear is supposed to have *killed* his mum. That's what he was in prison for before he escaped. If he hated her that much, surely this'd be the last place he'd want to visit?"

"Maybe he wants to apologise," Josh said. "Or spit on her grave. How do we know how the mind of a psychopath works?"

"Sometimes I'd love to know how *your* mind works..." Alice muttered.

In this new silence, Becky resumed gazing at the stars and latched back onto her initial train of thought... They all looked so tiny. Whoever had decided they were all as big as the sun was off his (or her) head. But it was what was between the stars that interested her even more: the blackness. Yes, she'd seen videos and listened to teachers' lectures about space, but it didn't seem to add up. All that darkness and nothing going on? How could they be sure? It was a perfect hiding place for anything. The sky could be teeming with life and no one would know.

Becky was "thinking big" again so she forced herself to stop. She was too tired for the big stuff. Just thinking the word 'tired' made her yawn... Never mind Joseph Fear's brain, she

103

figured her *own* would be worth someone analysing.

Upon her yawn, Josh asked for the time.

"Quarter to eleven," Becky replied after checking her watch. "We'd best be getting back."

No sooner had she finished talking than Josh's phone beeped. He read it and swore.

"What?"

"My parents have taken the car out."

"So you can't give me a lift home?" Becky asked, finding it hard to keep the frustration from her voice.

Josh shook his head.

"I'll walk you back though," he added hurriedly. Becky couldn't help notice Alice's eyebrows raise. Alice was of the strong opinion that Josh had hidden feelings for Becky that surpassed friendship. Becky was neither inclined to agree nor disagree.

"That'll take ages," she complained.

"Not if you go across the moor," Alice said.

Becky was apprehensive – the moors felt worryingly isolated on the brightest of days, which was why she usually got someone to drive her if she was going to the other side of the village, but she couldn't call her parents as they were away with Alice's. The walk across the moors was admittedly the most direct route to her house, taking about twenty minutes. If they went through the village it would be well over an hour.

"Done. We'll go across the moor," Josh said, standing up from the bench.

As he did so, Becky looked at him, as if taking him in for the first time. Josh was of average height, a pale complexion and was notably skinny. In fact, he looked like he might snap if he fell over. The more Becky thought about it, the less she could see the need for him to walk her home. If anything happened, it would probably be *her* protecting *him*...

"Would you like me to come with you too?" Alice asked, reading Becky's mind as she so often did.

"It's fine," Becky lied. "Josh'll be with me. Go home and I'll see you Monday."

The decision was made. They said goodbye and parted ways; Alice three hundred yards to her house, Becky and Josh over a mile across the moors.

As soon as they left the protective illumination of the park light, Becky felt unease wash over her. Here was the concealing darkness she had just been thinking about, only not in space; it was all around her. Oppressive. And now she couldn't help but let her mind wander and explore the possibilities of what it might conceal. When she really thought about it, it seemed there were more shadows than there were objects...

'Stop it!' she said to herself. *'You're making yourself paranoid.'*

Just as they reached the edge of the park, Becky thought she heard a slight crunching sound behind them. She turned her head and stared into the dark: nothing distinct, but she was almost positive she saw something dart away to the right into the trees. It was just too dark to be sure.

"What?" Josh said.

"I thought..."

"What?"

It could have been a tree in the wind, or an animal. There was no point making herself scared. They just needed to get home as quickly as possible.

"Nothing. It's nothing."

"Are you sure?"

"Yes," she snapped, perhaps harsher than she had intended. "Come on."

Becky led the way out of the park, through the gates and onto the moor. It was a downhill walk from then on, through the former marshland, towards the south end of the village. She could just make out the old church at the very bottom of the hill which signified the end of the moor and the start of civilisation again.

They continued downwards, the gradient of the hill allowing for a quicker descent. The grass grew to their knees and its contact with their jeans made a slight sibilant sound which filled the silence.

"S'gonna be a lot harder walking up this coming back," Josh said pointedly.

"You didn't have to walk me home," she replied, although they both knew that wasn't true.

"Yeah I did. It's less scary when you're with someone... I might crash at yours tonight and make my way back in the morning."

It was Becky's turn to raise her eyebrows. Maybe Alice was right. It wasn't explicitly a question, so she chose not to reply and carried on walking. A gust of wind sent her hair flying in all directions and she was glad she was wearing a thick hoodie – Josh must have been freezing in his thin Manchester City shirt.

About fifteen minutes after they had left the park, the hill started to flatten out again. They could see the church more clearly now, over the short stone wall and into the graveyard. The headstones stuck out from the ground at peculiar angles like a dentist's nightmare.

There was a sudden, distinct snapping sound behind them, like a twig being stepped on. Becky looked at Josh, and his face mirrored what must have been her expression. They both froze, but the thin sound of something moving through the grass continued from behind them for a second before stopping suddenly too.

Someone was following them.

They looked at each other again. Becky's heart rate began to accelerate. She turned around and stared into the blackness up the hill.

"Who's there!?" Josh shouted with little conviction. The accusation ricocheted back in a disturbing echo, the question reverted on themselves.

Still looking behind them, Becky took a step closer towards Josh, genuinely frightened. She felt a strange urge to clutch his arm, but knew it wouldn't help the situation. Going across the moor had been a stupid idea.

As the two of them squinted the way they had come, they saw a distinct shadow take a step forward from the darkness. It was barely a silhouette but looked threatening, if only because it was facing them, unresponsive to Josh's question.

The figure remained motionless for several long seconds. Becky stood paralysed as human features became more distinguishable.

Then it moved towards them.

They turned and ran, pounding their feet on the ground as they hurled themselves through the grass. It wasn't long before the hill completely flattened and they vaulted the small stone wall into the graveyard. They weaved between the headstones, sprinting in the direction of the church and the civilisation that lay on the other side of it.

Then the world disappeared from underneath them and they were falling, the sickening feeling of predicting an extra stair magnified a thousand times. There was a terrible cracking noise and Becky landed on top of Josh who yelled loudly in pain.

Now she was really panicking. Her heart was hammering on her rib cage in an uncontrollable frenzy. What the hell had just happened? Where were they? It was so dark...

She pushed herself up off the floor but her hand did not meet grass. Instead, it sunk into earth and she felt mud squash into her finger nails. As she stood up she realised that there were four solid walls of earth surrounding them – they had fallen down a deep hole in the ground. The top of the hole was about a foot above her head, making it impossible to pull herself up. They were trapped.

Becky began to tremble. She stared upwards at the edge of their prison, waiting for something to appear any moment. Nothing. Then she noticed that Josh was whimpering.

"Josh?"

Becky bent down and felt for her friend. Her hand met his head which was wet with blood. She felt under it and realised he had not landed on earth – a large flat rock had stopped his fall.

"Josh," she whispered in his ear. "Josh, can you hear me?"

She saw the shape of his head nod in the darkness.

"Josh, we've fallen down a hole. W-we need to get out before he finds us, but we need to keep quiet. You need to g-get up and help me."

Josh nodded again, but didn't move.

"Josh you need to get up," she said. "I'll help you."

She helped raise him from the sprawled position in which he lay and gently rested him against the side of the hole. The blood from his head wet her cheek as she did so, and he whimpered through short gasps and tears. She decided to leave him there for a few seconds while he got used to the pain.

"Come on Josh," her shaking voice

whispered after a short while, grabbing him by the hand and pulling him up. He pulled himself back down, groaning and clutching his head.

"Josh!" she hissed. "You've got to help me get us out of here!"

He didn't move.

Determined not to let panic completely consume her, Becky reached in her pocket for her phone. Remembering the shadow that lurked somewhere nearby, she put it and her head inside her hoodie so the light from the screen could not be noticed outside, and dialled 999.

"Emergency – what service do you require?"

"Police." The tiniest whisper.

"I'm sorry?"

"Police," she repeated, frantic but quiet.

"Was that police?"

Becky hung up the phone. She knew it would be impossible to describe where she was and what was happening whilst keeping her voice inaudible to someone who might be just five metres away.

Plan B: Remaining in the refuge of her

hoodie, Becky pressed '*Compose SMS*' on her phone. She began to type with her quivering fingers, worried that the simple clicking of keys would be enough to reveal their location: '*Fallen down hole near church at bottom of hill. Josh banged head. Someone else here. Please come help. Promise not joke.*'

She sent the message and set her phone to '*no alerts*' – whenever it vibrated it sounded like a power drill. Twenty seconds later, she saw the '*Incoming call*' screen and Alice's smiling caller image.

Becky pressed the red button and sent another text: '*Cant talk he wil no where we r*'

A minute later: '*On way*'

And so the wait began. Becky sat next to Josh, whispering in his ear that Alice was coming. He was mainly unresponsive, twitching only slightly to acknowledge he had heard her. She made a few futile stretches to try and judge how impossible getting out of the hole would be, but never physically attempted it, knowing that it would make too much noise. She then alternated between fearful glances at the top of the hole and squinting at her watch. Time seemed to be dragging the more she looked at the ticking hands, but it was easier than looking upwards.

Fifteen minutes had gone by now. Had Alice not run? Where was she?

As Becky wondered about the whereabouts of her friend, the moon freed itself from the tatters of black cloud and for the first time since they had been with Alice, there was ample light to see things.

She repressed a gasp as she saw the extent of the damage to Josh's head – there was a large cut that ran from his hairline, through his temple and down past his eye. The whole right side of his face was covered in blood and his eyes were shut tightly in pain.

She looked around the rest of the hole, which would have fit three more people at a push. The walls were very compact and it was perfectly square. But what really drew her attention was the blood spattered "rock" that Josh had fallen onto – a slightly cracked gravestone.

Had it been placed inside the hole after it was dug, or had it fallen in? Were they *in* a grave? The moonlit text on the stone sent a chill through Becky's body:

'IN MEMORY OF A WIFE AND MOTHER
ANDREA FEAR
DIED MARCH 2ND 1998'

Becky read the words again to work out why they had made her so uneasy.

Fear.

They were inside the freshly dug grave of–

For the first time, pure fear began to creep its way through her bones. They were in serious danger. And she had led Alice right into it. She was home alone while their parents were away – she would have come by herself. What if she'd already come?? What if she'd headed towards the graveyard and been intercepted by–

"Becky!"

Alice. Becky heard her friend's voice in the distance, but couldn't tell from which direction it came from.

"Becky! Josh!"

She was torn – should she shout and give away her position? Alice had been brave enough to give away *hers*. But Alice didn't know what was out there. It might take ages for her to help them out of the hole, enough time for–

Becky put her head back in her hoodie and called Alice on her mobile. It took two rings before she answered:

"Becky! Where are you??"

"We're about a quarter into the graveyard," Becky whispered, her shaking voice louder than before. "A hole in the middle if you're facing the very back of the church. Can you–"

The screaming from the phone ripped through Becky's ear.

"Alice?!"

Her friend's screams could be heard from a distance as well as through the mobile, the most horrible sound she had ever had to listen to.

"Alice?? Speak to me!"

She could hear something else down the phone through the screaming. A deep, heavy panting like a dog, but disturbingly human. Becky could do nothing but stand there and feel helpless until the call was cut off.

The helplessness continued after the screaming stopped.

"Josh!" Becky could hear the loud panic in her voice now but she didn't care – she just had to get to Alice. "Josh! He's got Alice!"

"W-what?"

Josh's head rolled back as he tried to take in what was being said. He was heavily concussed. Becky knew that he needed medical attention as of half an hour ago – he was going to be no help. She needed to get out, save Alice and find someone to help save Josh, before they all found themselves in their *own* graves.

Graves.

Finally appreciating the complex way her mind worked, Becky dropped to her knees and put her hands underneath Andrea Fear's gravestone, feeling Josh's wet blood on it as she did so. She put her feet against the side of the hole and pushed as hard as she could, heaving it into an upright position before wobbling it over to rest on the side: a perfect step to freedom.

"Josh, I'm coming back for you," she whispered, jumping onto the top of the headstone and out of the grave.

Now what? Becky stared around her in all directions, taking in the graveyard which was enveloped in a layer of mist, glowing in the new moonlight. Squinting through the darkness between the headstones, she struggled to find a sign of life. She memorised exactly where she was in relation to the church and the wall for when she returned, and sprinted off towards the other side of the graveyard where she thought Alice's screaming had come from.

"ALICE!" she shouted desperately, trampling through bracken. "ALICE! I'M COMING ALICE!"

In her haste, Becky tripped over the bottom of an aslant gravestone and landed painfully on her front in a patch of dishevelled heather. She pulled herself up, but as she did so, saw something small and white on the ground about five headstones away. She scrambled over, squatted down and saw one of the white Converse shoes Alice had been wearing that day. Becky's stomach lurched as she saw the thick dark liquid which covered the top of it.

She was too late.

Realising her shouting had already been louder than any possible phone call, Becky got her phone out from her pocket again, dialled 999 and responded "police and ambulance" to the operator's familiar question. She hurriedly described what had happened, only vaguely aware that tears were streaming from her eyes. She gave the most accurate description of where they were that she could, and was told that help would be with her as soon as possible. Not soon enough.

Once finished, Becky did the complete opposite of what the woman had advised and ran back towards the open grave. She had to get Josh to safety. It might not have been too late for Alice, but she didn't know where to start looking...

She drove the thoughts from her mind as she raced back, sweat and tears merging on her face. Constantly noting her location compared to the church, she retraced her journey until she found where she had come from, and looked down into the hole.

Her stomach churned as she saw the empty grave below her. In the moonlight, she could see the blood illuminated on Andrea Fear's headstone. A lot more of it than before she had left.

All was lost.

"JOSH! ALICE!" she shouted hopelessly, sprinting wildly through the graveyard now. She had no ideas, no plan, nothing. She had never felt so isolated and helpless before. "ALICE! JOSH! SOMEBODY!!"

She needed help. She couldn't do this by herself. Where were the police??

Becky pulled her phone from her pocket without deciding exactly who to call. Her mind raced through locals who may be able to help her, but she never made a decision: the screen told her she had a new message which she had not read because she had set her phone to *'no alerts'*.

Cursing her stupidity, Becky reread Alice's name on the screen to make sure she had read it right. She had:

'I escaped but injured next to the church cant call he might no where I am come quick'

Setting her phone back to *'vibrate'*, Becky's heart and legs were pounding again as she headed back across the graveyard towards the church. Elation and fear clawed at her for the emotional top spot as she ran: Alice was alive!

But she was not out of danger yet, and Josh could be anywhere – she had to be quick...

She could feel her energy weakening already – her wheezing breath was a dangerously loud sign that she had been running too much, and the stitch in her side screamed at her to stop and rest. *'No!'* she protested. *'I've got to save my friends!'*

The church stood at the bottom of the graveyard, the stained glass windows reflecting the moonlight and casting a red glow on the surrounding darkness. Fear won the battle as she arrived at the back entrance of the building – she was shaking uncontrollably now.

Becky resisted the urge to call out Alice's name – she could not give away their position; the attacker, who's name she refused to register, could be anywhere. She started to pace anticlockwise around the church, but as soon as she turned the first corner, she stepped on something hard and had to regain her balance to stop herself falling over. She bent down to see what it was, and recoiled instantly.

The bile rose to her throat and Becky vomited where she stood, unable to tear her eyes away from the abomination which now lay on its side. Its clumped blonde hair rested in a large pool of blood that was made only more terrible by the crimson reflection of the windows. Alice's blue eyes stared blankly up at Becky, tragically emotionless.

Tears, sweat and vomit were one, trying to expel the revulsion from Becky's head. She was on her knees, cradling her own head in her shaking hands, sobbing, retching, moaning. Her friend was dead. Alice was dead. Alice was–

Becky felt her phone buzz in her pocket and her sharp rapid breathing fell immediately. Trembling, she slowly pulled it out to see she had another message.

From Alice.

But Alice was in front of her. Alice was–

He must have had Alice's phone. How long had he had it? Had he sent the last message too? Had he led her here...?

As her shuddering fingers opened the message which simply read '*behind you*', Becky felt an unnerving hand grasp the edge of her shoulder...

Die Entartung

"<My Führer,>" Werner Haase's gaunt face looked almost manic as the plea escaped his lips. "<You know I will respect you and your judgement until the day I die. But you *must* reconsider. If you take your life tomorrow, everything you've accomplished up to now will mean nothing–>"

"<Haase, be realistic.>" Adolf Hitler turned his head away from his personal physician dismissively. He was sat behind a large wooden desk which was littered with papers of avid scribbling and diagrams. "<Steiner has lost us the war. It is over.>"

"<But–>"

"<No buts. Although I trust you and your suggested method of suicide, I want you to test the potency of one of the cyanide capsules on Blondi to ensure it is lethal, effective immediately.>" Blondi was Hitler's German Shepherd, given as a gift to him by Martin Bormann in 1941. "<It is your responsibility that

Eva and I die an instant death.>"

"<I *will* test the cyanide my Führer, but please hear what I have to say.>" His hands were beginning to shake, so he plunged them deep into his pockets before Hitler could tell.

Hitler sighed. "<What is it Haase?>"

"<I think there's a chance we can get you out of here, to continue your regime on another day.>"

"<No. I will stay in Berlin. There is no way to escape them forever. It is over.>"

"<What if you were disguised?>"

Hitler looked up into his physician's eyes clearly for the first time, as if he had only just noticed he was there, and was unimpressed with what he had found.

"<You think a wig and a pair of spectacles will stop them from shooting me where I stand? What is wrong with you Haase?>"

"<My Führer, I'm not talking about a few simple accessories. You *must* see what I've been working on – I think I am able to make you walk out of here in a completely new body, free to bring Germany to its natural glory on another day!>"

Hitler looked down again at the desk. At first glance he might have seemed quite nonchalant, but a slender furrowing had spawned on his forehead which was suggestive of deep, inner turmoil. Over ten seconds passed, and Haase opened his mouth to further his case, but closed it again upon an instructional raised hand. Finally, Hitler spoke:

"<If you were anyone but my very best physician, I would have you sent straight to the insanity ward. But I know from experience that your intellect is beyond measure, and you would not make these outlandish claims if you did not at least *believe* you could do what you say... show me what you had in mind.>"

Relief seemed to flood through Haase's face for a second, but soon it returned to its desperate state – he had only convinced Hitler to hear him out, not to go through with it. Haase led the way to his own office.

Apart from one clear pathway from the door to the desk, the room was crammed full of the physician's equipment. Everywhere you looked there were test tubes, models and copious stacks of books and papers. A large circular machine which looked like something from a science fiction film occupied one corner. The walls were plastered with huge diagrams of human anatomy, but they were covered with additional handwritten notes and drawings. A black cat sat on the desk amidst piles of papers, raising its head slightly as they walked in before looking down again at its outstretched paws.

Hitler raised his nose as he took in the unruly mess that was the doctors' quarters. Should he really trust a man who could not keep his room tidy?

"<Here...>" Haase said, striding to the desk, reaching behind it and pulling out a large birdcage. Inside the cage was a small brown monkey. It sat feebly at the bottom, clinging to the bars and staring sadly out at them. "<This is Benno. He's a rhesus macaque.>"

There was an awkward silence.

"<Haase,>" Hitler said, frustration evident in his tone as the lower half of his face tightened beneath his moustache. "<You are being paid a handsome fee to save the lives of wounded soldiers in the casualty station. If you've actually just been sitting here, stroking your pets->"

"<My Führer, that is the last thing I have been doing. I've... I think I...>" Haase seemed to be struggling to explain the brilliance of his supposed discovery. "<Just watch.>"

He opened the top drawer of his desk and removed a small tin box. Four twisting digits opened the lid, and inside were a number of bright orange syringes. He removed one and held it up to the light, checking for something. Satisfied, he opened the door of the birdcage which was resting on the desk next to the cat, and drew the needle close to the monkey. The creature cowered against the bars – apparently this was a process it was familiar with. It seemed too weak to be able to put up sufficient protest though, and Haase inserted the syringe gently into its side, releasing the orange liquid into its body.

"<I use a monkey,>" Haase explained as he injected the mysterious drug, "<because their genetic information is so similar to that of a human's. If it works on a monkey, it is likely to work on you.>"

"<*Likely?* Haase, I am no monkey for you to experiment on.>"

Haase either didn't hear Hitler or chose to ignore him. He lifted the cat, which hadn't flinched yet in the presence of the primate. It purred slightly as he stroked it gently from head to tail, cradling it like a baby. "<This is Margit. My pet and... volunteer.>"

Haase took another syringe from the container. Smiling down at the cat, he gently inserted the needle into its leg. The animal hissed slightly, and then was silent again. Haase placed it back on the desk next to the cage, before standing back to watch the two animals.

Twenty seconds passed before Hitler asked "<what in God's name are we supposed to be looking at?>"

"<You will see my Führer,>" Haase said. "<Any second now, you will see.>"

And he did. Not long after he spoke, the monkey began to twitch its head from side to side, clearly feeling some sort of internal agitation. Haase and Hitler drew closer to the cage and saw that beneath its hair, the skin had started to move slightly, as if being stretched back and forth by a strange invisible force. Ten seconds in, and it was bubbling like a pancake.

The monkey did not look in pain whilst this was happening, just confused, holding onto the bars of the cage.

"<What's happening?>" Hitler asked.

"<Its metabolism is changing... the genetic code is essentially being rewritten right in front of us. Watch!>"

Haase pointed to the cat which was now undergoing the same curious performance. The hair of both the animals soon started to stand on end, as if an electric current was running right through them. Hitler stared in bewilderment.

"<These are all just side effects of the real objective,>" Haase explained. "<The rest of the body just destabilises for a while, but the real wonders are going on inside the animals' brains.>"

He raced over to the circular machine in the corner of the room. He flicked a switch and a whirring sound started. Lights began to flash, and a tube protruding from the machine and disappearing somewhere behind a stack of books was suddenly filled with the same curious orange liquid.

"<Basically,>" Haase said, moving round

the machine and adjusting the controls as it began to vibrate, "<the subjects' brains have both been turned into biological transmitters and receivers. They are sending out organic signals on a frequency that no natural device can receive. This device I have made...>" (he paused for a few seconds whilst carefully adjusting a dial) "<...receives those signals, converts them both and sends them the opposite way.>"

He slammed a huge button on the side of the machine with a sense of finality. An increasingly loud whirring noise erupted from inside it, and the top began to open out like a small aircraft hangar. A large illuminated sphere extended from inside on a clear cylinder which contained more of the liquid. The sphere glowed even brighter, and the whirring noise settled to a constant loud humming.

The cat and the monkey both slumped where they were, unconscious, and the monkey let go of the bars. Their skin was still bubbling, but less vigorously now, and their eyes were closed. Hitler took a step back to watch the events unfold, undecided whether his leading physician was demonstrating a revolution years ahead of their time or an insanity hidden until now.

The machine's whirring stopped, and it groaned to a halt, pulling the sphere back inside itself. The lights on the side stayed on. The cat and the monkey slowly began to open their eyes.

"<Watch!>" Haase shouted, his face breaking into a gleeful grimace. He opened the cage, pulled out the monkey and placed it on the desk, prodding it a few times until it opened its eyes fully and slowly lifted itself up. It didn't pull itself into the sitting position it had been in inside the cage however – it put its weight on all four limbs, but seemed to have little control over them, as if it was using them for the first time. Haase put his hand underneath its tail and pushed it forwards, encouraging it to walk over the piles of papers which obviously held little importance to him compared to the current phenomenon. It struggled to put its feet down as it moved drunkenly and collapsed three steps into its journey, unsure of its own weight and how to balance itself.

Hitler's attention moved to the cat as it

awoke fully and began having a violent fit, as if panicking about something no one else could see. A series of spasms led to it rolling onto its back, twisting and flailing like an upturned beetle. It eventually pulled itself up again, but attempted to sit on just its back two legs, kicking upwards wildly with its front two as if it was swatting away an invisible fly.

"<They have swapped bodies,>" Haase said simply. "<The brain activity has transferred from one mammal to the other. What you see before you is the animals getting to grips with their new bodies. This is not the first time I have swapped them over, but they react similarly each time, and will remain like this until I reverse the process. It must be quite traumatic for them, but it won't be anything like this for you, as you would be entering the body of another human.>"

Again, Hitler did not speak. He just watched the two animals struggle to get to grips with the situation they had found themselves in. As he did, it was clear that what Haase was saying was true. They seemed to be genuinely struggling to work their limbs correctly, and were moving in a way that would have been more suited to the other animal. Incredibly, his physician had swapped their brains. Haase saw that Hitler was beginning to realise the magnitude of the discovery:

"<Now do you see? This science could be hundreds of years before its time... Just think! We can put you in the body of another human, so that you can escape. And then one day, you can try again, knowing what went wrong this time and not making the sa...>" (Haase corrected himself) "<not *allowing* the same problems to arise.>"

Hitler nodded slowly. It did make sense.

"<But whose body would I use?>" he asked. "<I'm not the only one they will kill as soon as look at.>"

"<Follow me,>" Haase said, and led Hitler from the room and down into the main casualty station which Haase had apparently not been spending as much time in as he should have been.

"<This,>" Haase said, taking Hitler into a small room which contained just one bed, "<is your new body. If you want it.>"

Haase pulled back the covers of the bed to reveal an unconscious man, strapped to the bed and wearing nothing but grey underwear. He was tall, extremely well built and had blonde hair. Haase lifted one of the man's eyelids to reveal a blue iris: the perfect Aryan.

"<I have been keeping him sedated,>" Haase said. "<He is a shell shocked soldier but of a perfect physical condition – I knew he was exactly what I... what *you* needed."

"<Let's try it. Let's practice now.>"

"<My Führer, the process will initially make you very weak. That's why Benno and Margit–>"

"<Do it on someone else first. Check it works on humans.>"

"<Surely it is best no one knows? Then the Soviets cannot torture the truth out of anyone?>"

"<I find that highly unlikely... but a trial run does seem quite fruitless at this late stage. I should be the first to try out your potion. If it works, it works. If it doesn't, it doesn't, and I will commit suicide as planned. Can you find a body for Eva too?>"

"<I'm afraid I cannot pinpoint the process yet. If you both took the serum at the same time, you would probably end up just swapping bodies with each other. If there is only you and the soldier in the equation, you can do nothing but take each other's place.>"

"<Yes,>" Hitler said. "<It shall happen tomorrow. Eva and I will prepare for suicide. You will do what you need to do with your machine and this man. I will inject myself and, if it works, I should find myself in this body within a minute. Are we agreed?>"

"Yes my Führer," Haase said, knowing that his brilliance was not to be congratulated and he should be thankful with this abrupt end to the showcase of his work – he had not expected Hitler to actually go along with it. "I envy how you create such clear, effective plans.>"

*

Hitler plunged the syringe deep into his thigh, emptying the orange liquid into his body.

"<Adolf? Adolf, what is that?>" Eva asked him.

"<This is... something Doctor Haase gave me to numb the pain.>"

She hardly seemed to hear his lie, walking around her husband's personal study distantly. She held the Walther PPK pistol at the ready in her shaking hand.

Hitler began to feel a warmth run through his body, as if his blood had just been heated up somehow. It was not painful, or even particularly uncomfortable, just slightly disconcerting. Then he felt his skin stretch oddly all across his body and his hands started to bubble just as the cat and the monkey's had done. Well, he'd managed his part of it – but had Haase managed *his*?

Two minutes of frantic anticipation and empty last words, and still no change. His skin was moving, but he felt completely rooted in his own body. It hadn't worked; they just had to end it.

"<Are you ready for this?>" he asked Eva.

She nodded, and reluctantly held the gun up, pointing it at the head of the man she had loved for so long. The cyanide capsule Hitler knew to be in her pocket, ready for her to bite into the moment she had shot him.

He was suddenly feeling very weak...

panic? He could feel the life quickly leaving his legs and his knees starting to buckle under his own weight... His vision began to blur and a blackness grew from the corners of his eyes.

Eva closed her eyes and gritted her teeth.

BANG!

*

Hitler's mind sparked into his first conscious thought: It had worked.

He instantly felt the difference in the proportions of the strapping Aryan – although his muscles felt weak, he could feel their potential under his new skin.

His whole body was aching considerably from the jump... or from the drugs Haase had been using to keep the man sedated. He did not have the strength to move any part of his body, and when he opened as much of his eyes as he could, all he could see was blurred grey – presumably the ceiling of the shelter.

Hitler decided he had been unconscious for at least a day – it felt a while since his last memories with Eva. Eva... Something inside him ached when he thought of his wife, and he hoped that their bodies had been disposed of before they were made a spectacle of. It was strange to think that his own body probably no longer existed, but he didn't really care. He was just grateful to Haase for the second chance.

Over the next several hours, Hitler fell in and out of consciousness. In his more alert moments he attempted to pull together some sort of plan: how he would leave the shelter, what the first stage in the second attempt at the New Order would be and if a second attempt was even possible. It was hard to hold together any definite train of thought however as his tired mind drifted to and from sleep. Only when he felt the floor turning upside down was Hitler brought to his senses, falling through the air before he landed on the cold, hard floor.

He jumped to his feet and looked up from where he had fallen. But he could not believe the first proper image that his new eyes were giving him: A huge soldier, three times his size, was stood above him, holding in his hand the object he must have just shaken Hitler from...

No...

"<Quick! Look what I've found!>" the soldier laughed, shouting to what must have been a comrade in another room through the door...

The same door that Hitler now bounded towards, pushing all four limbs off the hard floor, trying desperately to use them effectively for the first time. He felt himself tripping over his own feet. He managed to make it out of the door and into a room that he recognised to be Goebbells' office... only much bigger – could it be possible...?

He looked behind him and saw the large soldier pursuing him – he needed to be faster. He ran through the next door and a huge version of the conference room, his office, the sitting room, the bathroom... and into Eva's room. He scrambled his way up a chair and stared into the mirror on her cupboard, praying that he was wrong...

But he wasn't.

He did not listen to what was being said as he was lifted up and handed to someone else, location a blur as they took him from the room and through the bunker. What he had seen in the mirror was conclusive: nothing mattered anymore. In this new body he was nothing. Less than nothing – crippled and humiliated more than his own body ever could have been.

The war was over. Adolf Hitler was no more.

11 Years Later:

David drank the last of his tea, stood up and stretched. His round stomach pushed against his blue overalls as he did so, alarmingly tighter than it had felt before his week off work. He wiped the crumbs off his face and torso and decided he was going to have to cut down on the biscuits. He picked up the newspaper from the floor next to where he had just been sat, folded it in half and left it on the table for the next person on a break. He had to admit that staggering the shifts made the zoo run efficiently, although it did mean that he was rarely in the company of anyone else for more than the thirty second exchange window between jobs.

David pulled the crumpled mini-schedule from his pocket to double check where he had to go next – the schedules had changed slightly in his absence last week. The single word '*monkeys*' gave him all the direction he needed as he set off from the hut, his heavy boots crunching along the footpath as he walked.

As he went through the zoo, his straw-like hair hanging loosely by the sides of his face and his fingers caked slightly in mud, David couldn't help but feel proud to be part of it. The Tierpark Hagenbeck was founded by Carl Hagenbeck, the first man to introduce imitations of an animal's natural habitat into the modern zoo. It was full of extravagant, realistic habitats that not only provided a stunning place for people to visit, but also made the animals feel at home as much as was possible.

The Tierpark was lucky to even exist. It had been destroyed in the Allied bombing of Hamburg in 1943, with only a few animals managing to survive. Apparently some of the monkeys there now pre-dated the bombing, having lived through the destruction and rebuilding of the zoo.

As he got to their enclosure, David found it hard to believe that they had been there that long; they were still full of life as he walked through the grass, emptying out the bag of vegetables. When he finished distributing the food outside, he entered their indoor enclosure. Even though it was a beautiful summer's day, Adolf was in his usual corner.

As David walked towards him, he saw that he was not alone – Adolf was holding another monkey towards him and seemed to be urinating onto it.

"Adolf!" David shouted, interrupting the proceedings. Adolf stood back and the other monkey darted away...

This was not the first time David had seen Adolf doing this to another monkey who was more than happy to have things cut short – just how much power did he have over the others? And he might have been mistaken, but he was almost sure that this one was male...

"Unusual" was the nicest way of describing the monkey's behaviour since David had started working there eight years ago – it was his co-workers that had pointed out the swastika Adolf drew in the shavings every single day that had inspired his nickname. The drawings were much less frequent now, and bribery was the only way to elicit one:

"<Same as usual,>" David said, bending down next to Adolf. "<I'll start you off, you finish, and you can have your banana.>"

Adolf watched as the man drew the first crooked line of the familiar drawing. Originally, Adolf had used the drawings as a reminder to himself of something he was determined not to forget... but it had now slipped away. Whatever it was no longer seemed important, and now all he cared about was A) that he had just been interrupted from his favourite pastime, but also B) that there was a banana up for grabs...

He completed the drawing, creating an identical crooked line in the shavings that intersected the other one. He had no idea why this was so important to the man or what the drawing represented, but if it meant he could have a banana, he was more than happy to play along.

"<There we go,>" the man said, and tossed him a large banana from the bag before walking away out of the enclosure. Adolf got to work on peeling it, piercing the skin with his teeth and ripping the sides off with his hands and feet.

As he ate, he realised how lucky he was being able to complete the drawing – none of the others received a guaranteed banana every single day, and usually had to make do with vegetables. Adolf decided to walk outside to show off what he had been given, and let them know further how much power he had.

When he got outside however, things were different than they usually were. Adolf could feel the uneasy atmosphere among the other monkeys instantly; they were all stood on their back legs, their heads twitching from side to side, talking to each other...

What was going on? Although he could interpret their basic behaviours and mannerisms, Adolf still had trouble understanding exactly what the others were saying, especially in unusual situations such as this.

And suddenly, they were running. Adolf dropped his banana and followed them – where were they going? In a blur, they left the confines of their enclosure and jumped into the main zoo. Adolf was unclear exactly how they had escaped – had the man left something open when he had brought them food?

People were screaming as the monkeys charged through the zoo, looking for... what? What was the plan? Adolf did not have one, simply following the others as they bounded along the paths and swung through the zoo's trees, screaming wildly to each other as they moved.

Eventually, they reached the zoo's exit. Men were shouting at them to stop, but of course, only Adolf could even understand what they were saying. The rush didn't stop once they were outside the zoo, moving parallel to the road.

"<Where are we going?>" he tried to ask the monkeys running either side of him, but they did not respond – he could not really speak their language. And yet he could not speak German anymore either – the communications with the men who fed him had always been asymmetrical. He spoke in a series of noises that no one recognised – he had no language.

But he could speak German once couldn't he? That was why he could understand most of what they said. Why *had* he known German?

And why had he forgotten it? It was so hard to remember.

Some of the monkeys had broken away from the group now, climbing up various trees or lamp posts. Some continued to run forward, some ran off down other roads, some towards houses. They all seemed to be in groups of two or more, the bonds they had made within the enclosure evident.

The monkeys around Adolf ran off in another direction, but he did not follow them – he was not close to them. He was not close to any of them. For his entire time at the zoo, he had not tried to bond with any of the monkeys, only manipulating them into giving him what he needed. They would not want him with them now. He did not regret his attitude in the zoo, but it did pose a slight problem to him now – where should he go?

He detached himself from the few remaining monkeys still running ahead, bounded towards a house and clambered up and over the wooden garden fence. After landing in a flowerbed, Adolf sat himself against the other side of the fence, hidden behind a large green bush – he would stay here until he could decide what to do next.

He tried to weigh up his options, but he couldn't even think of any... what had been the *point* in escaping? Having been used to two meals a day, he would now have to learn to fend for himself and possibly hunt, or pull food from bins... it seemed like so much effort. Maybe he should just go back to the zoo...

But somehow, that felt wrong. Something inside Adolf told him that the zoo was not where he was meant to be, and that he should grasp this opportunity to escape with both hands. The zoo had changed him, repressed something important until he had forgotten it completely – who was he before this? He was sure that he had not lived there all his life, and that he had perhaps even been of some significance to the world, but as hard as he tried, he could not remember. It was like having a strand of banana stuck in one of your back teeth, impossible to pull out – so frustrating that Adolf clutched his head to his knees, wishing someone would appear and explain why he felt like this.

He stayed like this for a long time, his

fingers digging further and further towards bone as he clenched his skull in anger, trying desperately to remember. But his thoughts were interrupted by the barking of a dog from somewhere close. Adolf jumped to his feet behind the bush, ready to flee or defend himself, but it was not barking at him – it was barking to itself, being brought back to this house after a walk. Adolf peered from behind the bush to get a good look at the dog as it was walked to the glass porch door, and caught a glimpse of its beautiful brown reflection...

Blondi.

That was her – Blondi, his dog! What was she doing here?! Adolf stepped forward, ready to return to his old pet, but stopped himself: No – this wasn't Blondi. It was just a dog that looked like her. Blondi was dead.

The dog and its owner entered the house and the door was shut, but he was no longer aware of them – he was too busy thinking about the light that had just come on in his head: Blondi was dead? Why? For some reason, he knew that it was his fault Blondi was dead...

The cyanide capsule. He had had it tested

on Blondi to make sure it worked. And it had. But for what purpose? What had been so important that he would kill his old pet? A huge sadness welled up inside him and pulled with it the answer to his question: He may not have become close to any of the monkeys, but he *had* known love once. Eva. He had told her to ingest the cyanide – she was dead now.

But what about him, was *he* dead? He fought through fragments of the scene in his personal study – Eva holding the pistol to his head, the gunshot, and then nothing. She had shot him like he had asked. There was no coming back from that.

And yet here he was. He had survived. How?

Adolf jumped from the flowerbed and walked across the garden towards the door of the house. He stared at the reflection of his head and pulled back the hair that covered it, searching for a scar. Nothing.

His eyes dropped down to look at his face. This was not what Eva had looked like in the study when she shot him – she was a human, not a monkey. But he was a monkey wasn't he?

Why had he been in love with a human?

No. He wasn't a monkey.

He had made love to her. Her size. Her species... He was a man. That was why he had never bonded with the monkeys in the zoo, that was why he understood what the humans were saying, that was what spending years at the place had made him forget!

No. There was more. He knew it. He knew he held a significance greater than that of a normal human. Adolf fought back to what he had recovered from his past: Blondi, Eva, the scene in the study... *Why* had he asked her to kill him? How had he survived? Somehow his consciousness had been transferred into the body of a monkey.

With this conclusion, a rush of images started to sprout from nowhere in his head: The Aryan strapped to the bed – *which should have been injected with* – the bright orange liquid – *by* – Haase – *who kept a pet* – monkey... In a frenzy, his brain connected each image to the last like an electric current, using them to repair the knowledge of his final days. But it didn't stop there. The pieces continued backwards, rebuilding his old memories, ideas, opinions, reawakening synapses that had not been used in years.

Then everything was there again, as if the last eleven years had never happened. He did not have to strain at all to remember serving Germany in the First World War, his imprisonment in Landsberg, the Third Reich, and, most importantly, National Socialism.

How had this happened? Had the sedatives Haase had been using on the Aryan meant his brain was too dormant to swap with? Perhaps it was simply that the monkey's body had been closer, and still had some of the chemical in from Haase's experiments... Or maybe Haase had been unsuccessful in just putting the drug in the Aryan... But how *could* he have been? It was not a complicated task. Unless he had meant for this to happen...

He jumped when the glass (that he had forgotten he was staring into) swung backwards and the woman he had seen walking to the house opened the door. He made to run as she bent down towards him, but a quick look up at her face stopped him where he was. She had thick, dark curly hair. Dark skin. Dark eyes. A hooked nose...

She was a Jew.

Her expression was cautious, yet excited as she crouched down all the way to his level and looked him in the eyes.

"<Well, what have we got here?>" A patronising tone, even to an animal. He wanted nothing more than to spit in her face, but that would get him nowhere. "<You must have escaped from the zoo, mustn't you? Mustn't you?>" Did she seriously expect him to answer? "<Why don't you come inside? I'll ring the zoo and we'll get them to come and pick you up.>"

She stretched her arms out towards him, but he just stared at her, unsure what to do. She had mentioned the zoo... he didn't want to go back. But he couldn't just leave her here. It went against everything he stood for.

He put out his arms, allowing her to pick him up. She laughed, like someone would laugh at a baby doing something new. He was carried from the porch, through the house, and into the living room. He could see pictures on the mantelpiece of the woman and other people with similar features – her Jew family no doubt.

The German Shepherd he had seen before started barking from one corner, running over to where they stood. He clambered up onto her shoulders, as far away from it as possible.

"<It's ok!>" she said, rubbing him stupidly on his back. "<Sigrid is soft as anything. She wouldn't hurt a fly.>"

He was quite positive that Sigrid had never seen a monkey before, and didn't want to be the test subject to see how she interacted with one, so he didn't move. The Jew could see he was scared and carried him into another room – the kitchen – before closing the door.

"<There you are, she won't be able to open that.>" She set him down on the worktop, and stroked his back again. "<I'll get you some food, and then I'll ring the zoo and they can come and take you home.>" Did she seriously think he, a monkey, could understand her? How stupid *were* they?

She pulled a loaf of dark brown bread from a cupboard and a carving knife from a drawer. She cut off a big chunk, handed it to him, and reached in another cupboard for a large book.

After finding what she was looking for in what was presumably a phone directory, she walked over to the telephone which was stuck to the wall and started to dial the number.

She turned and smiled assuringly at him as she waited for someone to pick up the phone. Eventually, she started speaking, but he was not listening to her. There was only one thing he cared about at this moment, and it lay on the kitchen worktop halfway between where he was sat and she was stood, covered in breadcrumbs.

He quickly stood up, ran along the worktop and picked it up. He ran to the edge and hurled himself through the air, the blade raised in both his hands. Then he was still, hanging from the knife which had lodged firmly between the Jew's breasts. He looked up at her face, which stared back down at his in horror.

She made a disgusting choking noise and started to fall towards the floor. He managed to jump out of the way to avoid being crushed, but then bounded back on top of her quivering body. Blood trickled from her mouth and she feebly tried to clutch at the knife, but he made sure it stayed where it was by biting at her hands. He stared into her dark brown eyes until she was still.

He then ripped off her shirt (with considerable difficulty, due to the fact that she was lying down and had a knife sticking from her chest). When it was completely removed, he put his finger in the blood that was running down her chest and started to wipe it across her stomach in various directions. This was the first time in years he had understood what the drawing stood for, made even more satisfying by the fact that it was done in Jews' blood.

Before he was finished with her however, there was a large barking from the other room and he could see the dog growling at him through the glass door, his second interruption that day. It lunged at the door, and a large crack appeared in the glass – it was going to be joining him any second if he did not move.

He clambered up onto the worktop, leant over the sink and opened the large window into the garden – a quick and easy escape route. He turned and took one last look at the scene – the dog throwing itself at the door, the phone dangling loosely from the wall, the Jew on the floor with the bloody swastika on her stomach. Not a bad use of his time, considering he'd only been around properly for about ten minutes.

He jumped out of the window and into the night. The darkness had appeared very quickly, and it had started to rain heavily – did Germany know? Did it know that its saviour had returned, ready to bring about its true glory? He had been given a second chance to establish the New Order and he would not fail again. In the name of the fatherland, he would not fail.

Hitler was reborn.

Letting Go

Her hand in mine, we ascend the hill. Long amiable grass blades stroke at our legs without conviction as we climb, but it's not enough. Nothing is.

The journey here was long – a lifetime, cut short. Every step we take seems to take us another two back and progress becomes a distant enemy, taunting us from afar.

The clouds are finally beginning to part and the sun deliberates an appearance – a respectful pondering.

Marley sniffs and I squeeze her hand. I want to tell her about these hills: the lifetimes her mother and I spent carelessly ambling between their disjointed crevices – an exploration of unconditional beauty. Adam's swollen apple prevents me.

We draw up to the crest and are hit by wind, her godlike fingers exploring our persons from head to toe and back. She realises of course that we have nothing to hide, understands that we just want to be left alone.

So she dances away as quick as she came, leaving the two of us: father and child, at the top of the hill, staring bleakly out at the world from indefinable angles. It is all here, the entirety of the universe: me, Marley, and an exponential space. Begging to be filled.

We look at the urn, its presence only now apparent despite being the focal point of our journey. Our lives. Hesitantly, I place our hands inside to release the embodiment of our pain and love. Silent tears run down Marley's cheeks. This is premature. Am I ready for it?

Our hands fly up into the sky, and she expels herself around the world's hill. Her pieces form a scene from six months ago, and for the first time in this journey we meet *true* life: God's greatest creation has arrived.

"I like your dress Mummy."

"Thank you Marley. What do you like about it?"

"I like how red it is. Red is my favourite colour you know."

"Why's red your favourite colour?" I ask her.

"It's the colour of buses," Marley explains – the most obvious thing in the world.

"What's so great about buses?" I ask.

"I don't know really. They just look pretty. Especially the ones with two rows."

"Have you ever been on a bus Marley?" she asks.

"No, and I don't really want to. The driver won't know where all my friends live like you do."

Her mother laughs. "You're probably right. Now go and get yourself a drink from the machine before you dehydrate!"

"Ok," she says, picking up her empty glass and making her way towards the buffet.

"So, how are you enjoying your first cruise?" It's my turn to answer questions. "Are you having a nice time?"

"Yes," I reply. "Yes, it's great. I feel very relaxed. I've not been worrying about work, I get to see you more – I'd *nearly* say it was worth the money..."

"To hell with the money!" she says. "That's not what life is about. *This* is what it's about." She reaches across the table and holds my hand, staring into and through my eyes. Her voice is serious now. "Me and you. And Marley. The happiest family in the world. Living life." I nod. "Whatever happens in our lives, I want you to always be able to remember us the way we are now." I nod again. "Promise me?"

"...I promise."

"Oh – turn around, I think Marley wants you."

"Daddy look it's a butterfly!" Marley says, taking my hand and pulling me into now. She points at the sky as the last of the ashes fall away and a striking red insect darts nimbly above our heads. "Come on!"

And we're bounding after it, fighting against the blades now as we chase our colourful friend. Wonder fills my being as I race down the hill in pursuit of her vividness. I can feel Marley's hand itching to be free from mine, to chase even further the delicate creature that leads us. At first I struggle to hold on, but I know I can't maintain it.

So I let go.

Marley slows in pace and bends her head upwards to watch her in amazement, shooting through the clouds in a final display of radiance for her beloved audience.

We stand together, and wave goodbye.

Over The Rainbow

If you told me three years ago that I'd end up as an amateur actress performing small scale pantomimes at Christmas, I'd never have believed you. It's probably a sign of how well your acting career is going when every member of the audience can bring three friends without pre-booking tickets, and an old man's sneezes from row eight can clearly be heard onstage amidst the final applause. This is my life now, but it wasn't always like this.

I originally wanted to study English at the University of Birmingham. My predicted A Level grades brought me (and my English teacher, Mr Baxter) to the conclusion that this aspiration was likely to become reality when the results came through, so that was the only place I bothered applying to. However, a lonely night in and several glasses of Blue Nun later, I had sent an eager email with a few trivial questions about the course, and any reading I should do in preparation, to "the Birmingham of University," and I knew that my chances of studying anything there, especially English, had gone down the drain faster than the rest of the wine.

Three years later I found myself leaving the stage door of the Descant Theatre, the smallest performance venue in town, with my head down, my denim coat wrapped tightly around me and my bag firmly over my shoulder. Not that I was really expecting to be harassed by a clamour of admirers after that evening's poor turn-out. Ok, so I didn't quite radiate Judy Garland as I danced my way across the Velcro yellow brick road to the back of the shabby stage, but you'd think they'd have tried to advertise the thing a bit better.

I started to walk towards the centre of town. A cold wind snatched at my ankles and bit at my face. If only Birmingham knew I could use personification like that, they'd come crawling back on their hands and knees. The street lamps were draped in horrible plastic fairy lights, hanging parallel to all the main roads as they had been since November. I blame the Coke advert, although how a fizzy drinks company has obtained the power to decide when an international religious holiday starts, I have no idea.

I found myself in the market, scanning the area for my mum, who I was supposed to be meeting with after her shift at Barclays. I'd always been the clever one in the family, but you wouldn't be able to tell now: her in a great position at a leading bank with the potential to climb even higher, when the only climbing I was doing was onto the crappy hot air balloon at the crappy end of our crappy play.

My jealousy was replaced by gratitude when I spotted her and the two polystyrene cups in her hand, pumping steam into the cold air. I reminded myself not to run over when I saw them, and graciously sat down next to her before clasping the sweet heat source between my hands.

Before I knew it, the reason we'd met up soon fought its way to the surface: the frequently occurring "I bet my life is shitter than yours" competition that I so often won.

"So basically," I concluded, fifteen minutes later, "Ian seems to think that I don't love him anymore, and if I don't show him I do before the end of the week, he's probably going to dump me."

"Tricky one," Mum said, with a serious face. "You'll have to make sure you sleep with him before the week's up."

"What, to show him I love him?" I asked.

"No, to get one more in before he dumps you."

I'm lucky to have such a supportive family.

"But I want to make sure he *doesn't* dump me!" I told her.

"Sally, I thought you were convinced he's sleeping with this Debbie anyway?"

"Well, yes but... well, no he's not... well I don't think he is, but if we *do* split up then it's more likely to happen isn't it?"

"...If you say so. Why do you think she fancies him again?"

I sighed, but resisted the temptation to ask who she'd been listening to for the last quarter of an hour, knowing she'd listened to everything I'd said. She just didn't understand. Maybe I didn't either.

"Just the way she looks at him whenever they're together. Plus she texts him a lot. I mean

I know they work together, but–"

"Why don't you go to one of their performances? See what's really going on?"

I looked at her with resentment in my face. I wanted to spend as little time as possible near that theatre and the people who worked there.

"Plus, if nothing *is* going on, you're supporting Ian and showing him you love him, which you've got to do anyway. In my eyes, that's two birds with one stone."

"Yeah... yeah you're right. It's probably not a terrible idea."

"There we are. When's your next night off?"

"Well, we're only doing a matinee tomorrow for the schools, so I guess I could go tomorrow night. It's their last show before Christmas."

"That's settled then. Let me know how it goes."

*

"Shit!"

"What?" Toby asked as we left the stage to half-hearted clapping. He had already tugged off the bristly mane that was velcroed around

166

his shoulders, and was unbuttoning his tight brown joggers.

I pointed to my right foot. The heel of the ruby slipper looked like it was hanging by a thread, causing me to walk on the toes of that foot, hobbling along like a war veteran. (There's a simile for you Birmingham.)

"Shit," he said, looking up again as he started to wipe the painted whiskers off his face. "How'd you do that?"

"I caught it in the crack at the bottom of that ****ing hot air balloon. I swear, if health and safety came to this show, they'd shut us down before we could even get our costumes off."

Sadly, they didn't come, and five minutes later, my costume was off and shoved in the corner of the dressing room I shared with the other two female cast members. I put both of the shoes in my bag, remembering in my contract there being a section about paying for damaged costume and props. "Stingy Steve", the director, would be only too happy to give me a three figure bill for a pair of glorified red pumps, so I knew I'd have to replace them before he noticed.

I left the stage door with my head down as

usual, but it rose again when I saw Toby and Frank leaning against the wall in a cloud of smoke.

"Guys, what the hell are you doing?"

"What?" Frank looked nonchalant.

"It's three o'clock for Godsake. Those kids could walk round here at any moment and see the Tin Man and the Cowardly Lion with a joint each. Have you not got *any* sense of decorum?"

"Nah, we don't do decorum," Frank winked at Toby. "Only pot!"

"Hilarious."

I left them to their spliffs, hoping that a policeman would get lost and end up in our part of town. A twenty minute walk and a cigarette later (hey, at least mine's legal), and I was at the crappy costume shop. The guy behind the till looked like his only ambition as a child had been not to work in a crappy costume shop. I could empathise.

"Hi, I'm looking for a pair of ruby slippers."

"Ruby slippers?"

"That's right."

"What for?"

"For… wearing?"

"I see. Let me have a look in the catalogue."

He opened a book that I, as an occasional Argos customer, would not have described as a catalogue. It had fifty pages at best and I was already dubious about it having a shoe section, let alone a pair of shoes that a budding Dorothy could wear.

"Is it for anything in particular?" the guy asked, clearly trying to remain friendly before giving me the bad news.

"I'm playing Dorothy in *The Wizard of Oz*." I lifted the demolished shoe from my bag. "And I've broken my shoe."

"No way!" the guy said, his face lighting up as he closed the catalogue completely to start what he clearly considered a potentially engaging conversation. "I went to watch it last week with the family! You were all very good!" Well, maybe he wasn't so bad after all… "So what happened to your shoe?"

"I, er… broke it. I got it caught in the bottom of the hot air balloon."

"Oh my god. I'm surprised things like that happen in such a large scale production."

"It's not really all that big…"

"I heard it was the biggest theatre in England outside of London."

He had seen a different show. He'd been to see the one that Ian and Debbie were performing in – the bigger, better… safer *Wizard of Oz*.

"Actually," he said, staring blatantly at my chest. "I don't think it *was* you who I saw. I must have seen it at a different theatre."

Add "boobier" to the list of comparative adjectives the other play has over ours. And Mum wonders why I'm insecure about Ian being in a show with the wonderful Debbie.

I left the shop two minutes later with a pair of ruby slippers. One had a broken heel. The guy had concluded that this kind of thing had to be custom-made, and as I had less than twenty four hours before the next performance, this was obviously no good to me.

After a while of wandering aimlessly around town looking for a man with a sign saying *'half price ruby slippers'*, I took the metro over to the Lowry theatre. When I got there and took in the beautiful building, I felt a sickening sense of déjà-vu. Last Christmas, back when my acting career had credibility, I would have arrived here to perform at, as the cretin had said, the biggest theatre in England outside of London. It was here I'd met Ian, one year ago, in *Peter Pan*. A romance between Peter and his fairy.

My relationship with Ian was the only thing from that briefly successful period of my life that had not come crashing down (yet). No one knew what to make of my spectacular trip through the imaginary wall of the Darlings' house, with my legs landing at unfortunate angles which revealed to the audience that I had decided not to wear the colour co-ordinated underwear I'd been instructed to – apparently pink G-strings do not appear in Tinkerbell's wardrobe. I've been told it wasn't that though which got me the sack from the Pelé Productions theatre group, but how I then decided that walking all the way around the outside of the house and entering the room again through the official doorway was the best way to cover up my mistake and retain my acting integrity. Personally, I would argue that it is always best to maintain the illusion of the set, but I've heard too many counter arguments to voice this anymore...

The fact that I was now on my way towards a theatre company which consisted of everyone that had been present at my sacking was testament to how much I liked Ian. I knew that if I went out with them all after the show, which I supposed was inevitable as it was their last show before Christmas, as nice as they'd be to my face, there'd be enough G-string jokes out of earshot to sink a Jolly Roger.

But I didn't hate them. It wasn't their fault I couldn't walk round a stage in a green slut costume without falling over myself. The only person I did have any real resentment for was Debbie. Throughout their current play, (an improved version of ours in every way – the kids playing the Munchkins in theirs remembered their lines for a kick-off) I couldn't help but think that Dorothy (Debbie) was touching the scarecrow (Ian) far too much. She really seemed to push herself onto him whilst helping him off his pole, was only too eager to grab his hand when the Cowardly Lion "frightened" her and had her arm tightly round his shoulder throughout the entire applause. Every time they made contact, my stomach clenched.

After the show, I went backstage to find Ian. Even that took some effort – with a chest like mine you have to be well versed in rhetoric when it comes to convincing security to let you in, but I eventually made my way to the same dressing room he had had last year that I remembered only too well.

Empty. But the play had been finished at least ten minutes, and I'd have met him on the way out had he already left. Where could he b–

No. Surely not...?

I marched my way down the corridor until I found the room with her name on – mine from last year. The new model. Hoping I was wrong, I barged open the door.

This was empty too. The room, lined with illuminated mirrors, curled round like a snail shell as I remembered it from my brief days of sprinkling fairy dust, and I followed it round to the shower that slotted into the corner.

As I did so, I heard the door open and a woman speaking. Instead of doing something logical, for example telling her I was looking for Ian and had got the wrong room, instinct kicked in, and before I knew it I'd jumped into the shower and pulled the curtain across my face. Sometimes I think there's a part of me deep down that likes getting herself into ridiculously tight situations, and if I ever come across her we'll be having words.

"–think he definitely likes me too." ... "Well we've been in this play together haven't we and one thing's kind of led to another and... yeah. Well I'm going to ask him to come over to the flat tonight..." ... "Yeah. Thanks. Well listen I've got to go now, but I'll give you a text later. Yeah ok. Bye... bye."

Through the gap between the shower curtain and the wall, I watched her put down the phone and take off her Dorothy costume. Wow. I really did have something to worry about. She looked even better naked than in her form-fitting blue dress. My heart started to pound as I realised that if she caught me now, there was absolutely no explanation, power of rhetoric or no power of rhetoric – I'd have "lesbian stalker" to add to my convictions.

She got dressed into a low cut black T-shirt and a pair of tight jeans. Slut. She left her costume strewn on the floor where she'd dropped it, presumably for someone else to pick up, and strutted out of the room.

I waited ten seconds to make sure she'd definitely gone before making my way towards the door, ready for a quick, confident exit. Just before I pushed down on the handle though, something red on the floor smiled innocently at me in the mirror.

A ruby slipper.

Now, I don't consider myself a bad person. I've rarely thought about stealing anything – it's just not in my nature. But as Mr Baxter once told me, there's always an exception to the rule, and that's how I convinced myself that what I was doing wasn't wrong as I scooped up the shoes and loaded them into my bag. They fit perfectly, as if the bag had been made specifically for this. It was fate.

My glee at solving the shoe issue disappeared quickly when I thought back to Debbie's phone conversation, which had pretty much confirmed my suspicions regarding her and my boyfriend. But I wasn't just going to let her take him from me...

I found Ian, now in his dressing room after a chat with David, the director. I couldn't help but feel slightly pleased to see him, even though I knew what he might have done/could be doing. He seemed surprised but pleased to see me, and I told him how well he'd done as I helped him take his Scarecrow suit off.

"How come you came?"

"...I just thought I'd show a bit of support."

"Well thanks. It's nice of you. Are you gonna come out with us all in a few minutes? I don't know where we're going yet, but it should be a laugh."

"...Yeah sure."

"You're not too embarrassed about what happened last year?"

"Of course I am, but I'm sure none of them will mention it!"

*

"So Sally... fallen through any invisible walls lately?"

Well they weren't talking about me behind my back, I'll give them that much. I just smiled back at Joe, now out of his Tin Man costume, who I had always actually gotten on with last year. I guess he was just trying to lighten the atmosphere, but as soon as he finished speaking an awkward quiet erupted across our table, even in the busy bar in which we sat.

"Sally, what do you do for a living?" Debbie asked me, flashing an annoyingly fake smile and sipping her cocktail with unbelievable self-importance. She knew what I did. She wasn't going to be stealing someone's feller without checking she wasn't a copper or a black belt in karate first. She knew that my job was just a shitter version of hers.

"I'm an actor too," I told her politely. "Not to the same scale as you of course."

"Are you working on anything at the moment?"

"I'm in *The Wizard of Oz* too actually. At the Descant Theatre?"

I knew she'd heard of it. I knew for a fact she lived ten minutes away. But of course, she pretended she hadn't heard of it, to highlight how small and shit it was. Just like she pretended she didn't know I was also playing

Dorothy. Just like she had pretended that every drab comment Ian had made all night was hilarious so she could wet herself laughing repeatedly.

"Can't say I know that one, but to be honest, I'm a bit of an amateur to the whole theatre scene myself. I was just lucky to join Pelé last year because of a sudden reservation."

Everyone else looked away, knowing what she had said, just like I did, just like she did. They probably knew what was going on between her and Ian as well, thinking I was the only one who didn't know. Thinking I was ignorant to the whole thing.

The night went on. I worked my way through the bar's collection of Smirnoff Ices. I started dancing – people I knew, people I didn't know, people I wasn't sure whether I knew or not. Everyone started to get a bit fuzzy round the edges. Except Ian and Debbie. They started dancing suspiciously close to each other and I started to feel ill so I grabbed my bag and headed to the ladies. Once there, I gripped the toilet seat with both hands. It *felt* still, but it still persisted on spinning round in circles, making me feel worse and worse...

I left the toilets five minutes later thinking I'd seen the worst of it, but felt even sicker straight away:

To the left of me, was the slim, slutty figure of Debbie in her ridiculously tight black top and jeans. If that wasn't enough to make me gag, she was currently eating the face off a figure she had pinned to the wall. A figure that could only have been one person.

I dropped my bag, reached for something hard inside and with my other hand, grabbed a fistful of her hair which I used to pull her from my boyfriend. She fell to the floor, screaming and I landed on top of her, clawing at her face with my free hand.

"WHAT THE **** ARE YOU DOING??" she screamed, attempting to get up.

"WHAT THE **** AM *I* DOING? I'M–"

"Sally?"

I looked up and saw Ian had come round the corner into the corridor, a bewildered expression plastered across his face. But if he was there, then who–

I turned my head to the wall and saw Chris,

the Cowardly Lion, leaning against it, looking more cowardly than I'd ever seen him.

"Debbie," I said, frozen on top of her. "I am so, *so* sorry. I thought that you were–"

"Is that what I think it is?" she asked, indicating towards what I had grabbed from my handbag and was now holding above her head, ready to strike her for a crime she had never committed.

I looked up at my weapon. The blood-red sequins winked at me in the artificial light.

*

My mum placed a second hot water bottle under my quilt. She walked through the mess of empty Ferrero Rocher wrappers, sat on the other sofa and turned Loose Women down two blips.

"You're better off without him you know," she said.

"No," I sniffed, pulling out another tissue from the box waiting loyally on the arm of the sofa before blowing my nose again. "I was wrong. There was nothing going on between him and Debbie."

"That may be true," she said, "but you're still better off without him. You're kind, you're funny and you're stunning. You could have anyone you want."

I shook my head and sniffed again.

"Come here," she said, joining me under the quilt on my sofa and putting her arm around me.

We carried on watching Loose Women. I wasn't paying any attention to what was being said though; I didn't really know the man they were interviewing/drooling over this week…

Eventually the programme finished and the credits came on. Mum turned the channel over before staring in disbelief at what had come on.

"–just then, the witch, to satisfy an itch, went flying on her broomstick thumbing for a hitch!"

I felt her head turn to look at me worriedly, unsure what my reaction would be.

"And oh, what happened then was rich!"

I don't know whether it was the ludic quality of the song, my mum's owl-like head movement or the impossible irony of this film being the one Channel 4 had decided to play on today of all days, but I felt the corners of my lips start to pull.

"The house began to pitch, the kitchen took a slitch…"

And suddenly I was laughing. It couldn't be helped. It was funny. It shouldn't have been, but it was.

"…it landed on the wicked witch in the middle of a ditch…"

My mum was laughing too, now she knew I wasn't offended. Now she had cheered me up more than any innuendo the loose women could have come up with without even trying. It was only funny because she was there.

"…whiiiiiiich was not a healthy siiiiituation for… the wicked witch."

Still laughing, I gratefully picked up my brew from the floor and began to put things into perspective: as bad as this week had been, as depressed as I was with no boyfriend and probably no job when I was reported to the union for theft, I knew that I was lucky to be where I was.

There's no place like home.

Next Genesis

"Ladies and gentlemen. People of America. There has been a lot of confusion and media hype over the last few months regarding a rapid change in the evolution of mankind as we know it. There have been reports across the United States about people who are able to perform highly abnormal feats, such as manipulating communication devices, imposing thoughts upon others and literally vanishing from sight.

"I am here to confirm that the rumours are in fact true. These people do exist. We have been in contact with a number of them, and they are currently assisting us in the exploration of this phenomenon.

"The origin of their newfound abilities is unclear to us and to them. We do not know for sure if this *is* simply a drastic leap in the evolutionary ladder, or, more likely, the product of an illegal, man-made experiment. America's leading scientific minds are working together to uncover the origins of this biological conundrum, but there have been no significant breakthroughs as of yet.

"What we *have* found, however, is a cure. These people have been dubbed 'mutates' and portrayed in the media under an extremely negative light. This is wrong. They are people, just like us, who are not to blame for their own terrible condition. Their affliction is nothing more than a disease. A corruption of healthy cellular activity, be it man-made or not, and it is our responsibility to help them counter that.

"Not only is mutation wrong on an individual, biological level, but we must also think about our country's safety. National security will always be one of our main priorities. Accommodating citizens who are able to resist military power, and possibly control our very thoughts, makes for a potentially apocalyptic future which we simply cannot entertain.

"We have developed an antibody designed to permanently suppress the corrupted genome. It will be issued to all sufferers without exception. Some people's mutation may take time to manifest, to the extent that they won't even know they have it yet. And it is for that reason that we will come directly to everyone with the disease.

"We have created a unique tracking device which allows us to locate anyone with the mutated gene. The specifics of how it works are of course confidential to prevent any attempts at sabotage, however it is an extremely efficient and effective means of locating the sufferers. Over the next few months, we will reach every single person with the illness, and issue them with the cure.

"The future is not lost. If we put an end to the problem before it begins, we can ensure that–"

Evie turned the President off, wondering if she had woken up in a dystopian sci-fi movie. Hearing reports on the radio about people being able to breathe underwater was one thing, but when the President publicly announced yesterday that there is a whole host of people who could do things she couldn't... well it just didn't bear thinking about. Having the statement constantly repeat on TV since then did nothing to reduce panic levels either.

Whether it was ethical or not, Evie thought the cure he had mentioned sounded like a good idea. There are enough murderers and rapists in the world as it is without half of them being able to walk through walls.

She picked her bag up and left the house, taking good care to lock the door. She was glad she lived so close to school so the journey of imagining people breathing fire and shooting electric bolts from their eyes could only last ten minutes. Hoping she would be able to forget about it in class and concentrate on her upcoming math final, she walked into school.

She managed to cast the mutates out of her mind for most of the lesson. Yes, it was the only thing anyone could talk about, but she had bigger concerns – Mr Anderson had put her next to Mark Crowley who was (unfortunately) her best friend's boyfriend.

Five minutes in and she was doing what she did multiple times a week: picturing what could have happened if she'd had the spine to ask him out before he had gotten interested in Rosie. She could picture him walking *her* to school every day. Them walking the dogs together in the park afterwards. Him going round to her's to watch a movie. The two of them sat on the bed together. Him leaning over for a kiss...

Evie sighed. She had really messed up. She looked at Mark across the desk, and for a fraction of a second, they made eye contact.

And suddenly, she was back in the perfect world with him. But it was different. It was so vivid. She could see every tiny detail like she was actually there. She could hear his exact voice saying her name, but in a way he had never said it before. She could feel his breath on her neck, the taste of his lips. It was real.

But it wasn't! She was sat in math, daydreaming!

But daydreams weren't like this; this was perfect. She could feel him pull at her clothes, push his body against hers... no! This was wrong! Andy was seeing *Rosie*. He would never – this wasn't right!

Feeling like she was throwing away the most precious thing in the world, Evie ripped herself from the fantasy, and found herself, clothed again, back in the classroom. Nothing had changed. Mr Anderson was still stood at the interactive whiteboard, poking numbers with a pen. The girls on the back were still whispering about mutates. Mark was still sat next to her... staring at her with his mouth wide open.

He knew. He had just experienced what she had. What the actual–

As she quickly turned her head from Mark, the words of the President from that morning echoed in her ears: "People who are able to perform highly abnormal feats... imposing thoughts upon others... mutates."

No. Surely not.

How else could you explain it?

Mark was a mutate. He had created the scene in his head and forced her to take part. He'd mentally made them have sex in the middle of a math lesson. Why would he do that? He didn't even flirt with her anymore like he used to. Like he still did with other girls. He was seeing Rosie, Evie's best friend. This was seriously messed up.

Evie stared at Mr Anderson, unsure whether to confront Mark now or after the lesson.

Mark made the decision for her and leaned close to her, a dangerously similar distance as he was in the dream, before whispering: "what the **** did you just do to me?"

She stared at him, dumbfounded.

"Me??? I..."

Evie stopped herself, and thought about it. She'd been thinking about him before it had happened. *She* fancied *him*. And they had been in *her* bedroom. He had never been in her room before – how would he know what it looked like?

She stood up from her chair, knocking things off the desk as she did so. Everyone in the class turned to stare at her as she picked up her things from the floor and stuffed them in her bag.

"Evie?" Mr Anderson asked as she walked towards the door. "Evie where are you going?"

She mumbled something about not feeling well, and before she knew it, she was running: down the corridor, across the field, down the road, home.

She ran up the stairs and collapsed onto her bed, tears dripping from her chin. She didn't know how frightened to be – what did this mean? What was going to happen? She had no idea. She needed to talk to someone.

Philippa.

She held the 'P' button on her phone, and the speed dial started ringing her sister.

"Hey sis, what's up?"

"Philly I... I need to talk to you," Evie whispered, her voice trembling.

"Well, I'm at work. Can I speak to you tonight?"

"Philly, I think I'm a mutate."

"...I'll be home in ten minutes."

Philippa put down the phone and went next door to see her boss.

"Darren, I've just been told about a family emergency. Is it alright if I–?"

"Yes, you get off," he said without looking up. "I hope everything's alright."

"I'll be back tomorrow," she said.

She left the room, collected her stuff and walked through the bank, which was pretty much dead. Recession. As she left the door, she passed a guy wearing a black balaclava and a leather jacket. This could mean trouble, but she would be no help and she had to get home to Evie, so she walked quickly down the road towards her car.

The boy in the balaclava walked to the cashier's desk.

"Sorry sir, I'm going to have to ask you to remove the balaclava. It's bank policy to–"

"I don't want to hurt you," he said, a slightly shaking hand pulling a pistol from his jacket and pointing it towards the cashier. "I want ten thousand dollars, in cash, in a bag, and you'll never see me again, I swear."

Adam could see his reflection in the glass between the two of them and nearly did a double take. He looked like a thug in a Batman movie. But *they* had all become the bad guys yesterday with the President's little announcement. "*A disease*"… It made him feel sick. In his reflection he could only see his eyes beneath the black balaclava, and that was all he would need. That and the glass.

The girl on the other side of the window, who was notably attractive, began to tremble.

"I… I don't… I…"

She looked to either side at her colleagues,

who were equally as shocked. Adam was pressed for time – he had to hurry things along. He moved the gun to the gap at the bottom of the window where the transactions occurred and pointed it through the hole towards them.

"I've not got all day," he said. God, this felt wrong. "Ten thousand dollars."

"Sir, we've not got–"

"Bull *shit*. You've got *it*, and you've got one minute."

As she moved back to try and assemble the money, Adam wondered again if he was doing the right thing. Of course he was – he needed the money to get out of the States. Why should he be forced to change his own DNA just because it was more advanced than that of those making the rules? He had to get away from the country, so he could keep his power. They'd given him no choice.

The girl was back at the window: "We've got the money."

"Where is it?"

"Someone's bringing it round to you."

He turned around, and an older lady walked towards him, carrying a large brown sack. So they actually looked like that in real life? Now he really *did* feel like a bank robber.

She placed the bag at his feet and stepped a metre away from him. He opened it and looked inside. Wow. That was a lot of paper. He looked up at the woman and saw her looking at him expectantly, awaiting approval – she wanted to know if it was enough. But he had no idea what ten grand looked like...

"That's right," he said, realising he'd look like a mug if they'd only put two in. "Thank you for the... cooperation. I–"

There was a large shattering sound from behind him. Adam turned his head and saw the glass from the cashier's desk scattering across the floor. There went *that* escape route.

"DON'T GIVE HIM THAT MONEY!" a middle aged man, presumably the manager, shouted from behind the counter, holding a shotgun and pointing it towards Adam. "Do you have any idea who you're stealing from you little shit? Do you really think we'll let you just walk out of here with our money?"

Adam didn't let go of the gun, keeping it by his side, but his heart started pounding and he began to shake. This was something he was not prepared for.

"You can't walk away from this. Put down the gun," the man said.

What now? He was caught before he'd even begun.

No. There was still a chance. He had an advantage over everyone in the room. He was special. If anyone could get out of this, it was him.

"I will," he said, as confidently as he could manage. "If I can have... a mirror."

"What do you mean, a *mirror*?" the man barked.

"They're glass coated reflective surfaces that–" he taunted, sounding a thousand times more sure of himself than he was.

"I know what a ****ing mirror is. But wh–"

"I just want a mirror. That's all I want. You can have your money, I'll put the gun down and I'll wait here while you call the cops. But I want a mirror."

The man was clearly struggling to get his head round this request. However, keeping the gun trained on Adam, he spoke to his staff:

"Who's got a ****ing mirror?"

Silence for a second before a timid voice said "I do." The hot girl Adam had spoken to first. She pulled a small handheld mirror from her pocket.

"Bring it to him," her boss ordered.

Hesitantly, she went round the back and a few seconds later, appeared from a side door, clutching the mirror.

"Thank you," Adam said, as she handed it to him, blowing her a kiss that even he hadn't expected. "You've really been the highlight of my day."

He took a few steps back towards the other woman who was stood by the sack of money and threw his gun to one side. That should take the pressure off. All he had to do now was escape.

"Pick that up," the man said to the older woman. "He's going nowhere until the police get here."

As she turned to pick the gun up, Adam dived towards the sack. He grabbed hold of the top of it, and with his other hand, snapped open the mirror and gazed into it.

The bankers watched as Adam and the sack were sucked into the mirror, which fell out of his now absent hand and clattered onto the floor. Before he disappeared, he heard a loud gunshot from the direction of the cashier's desk and a scream from behind him – the bank manager had hit one of his staff.

The screaming continued as Adam was hit with a blue light and a sink: he had appeared through a public toilet mirror... which a woman was using to adjust her makeup.

He climbed wearily off the sink and told her to keep calm, but she ran, still screaming, from the room. This was not good – he needed to lay low for a few minutes and regain his strength. Presumably the bank had already called the police, so he couldn't go out into the main street wearing a balaclava and carrying a sack of money...

The light was coming from a translucent window in the top left corner of the room. Adam went into the far cubicle, stood on top of the toilet and pulled it open – he would have to use it as an escape route the traditional way while he built his strength back up. He pulled himself onto the thin window ledge and heaved the bag through with him.

Ah. He was two storeys up. But someone would be back any second because of the screaming woman... Adam let go of the bag so it fell into the alley below, and before he could think to change his mind, dropped from the window, landing on his prize. It hurt more than he had expected.

There was no one in the alleyway and he was very out of breath, so he decided to stay sat down for a few seconds, taking his balaclava off then he could feel the air on his face. Why did using his power tire him out so easily? He felt like he'd just run a marathon. With one foot. Ok, he had just broken the conventions of the three dimensional world in which he lived and teleported half way across town, but after months of practice, he thought he would have been getting used to it by now.

As he regained his breath, he started to hear a noise. A sickening grinding sound which just emanated threat as it grew louder. Adam looked up and saw to his horror a small black helicopter descending towards him. How the hell had they found him so quickly?

Before he knew what to do, a spotlight had protruded from the chopper and he was dosed in a brilliant green light.

"Yep, that's definitely him," a voice sounded from an electronic device above. Adam's mind whirred and panic really started to set in: they'd only said that after he'd been caught in the light. Could this be the tracking device the President had spoken about? Already?

He picked up the cash and started to run. He didn't have the energy to teleport yet, so now it really was time for that marathon. Sprinting down the alleyway, he realised that this was to be the "make or break" moment in his life: If he escaped, he was out of the States and he wouldn't have to worry about them stealing his biological identity. If he was caught... well then he was not just a nobody; he was a nobody in prison for robbing a bank.

Just before he moved into the next alleyway, he glanced over his shoulder and saw several dark figures descending from the helicopter on ropes. Adam's feet pounded along the ground as he raced through two more alleys, his mind frantically grasping at potential ideas for a plan... He needed to get into the middle of town; it'd be hard for them to find him then.

Already a stitch had begun to formulate in his side, beads of sweat dripping from his head and his breathing growing even worse than it had been after the jump. He ripped his jacket off and left it in the alley behind him. As he did, he passed an open door which was surrounded by tables and boxes. One glance back inside told him it was a kitchen for a café. Decision made.

He hurtled into the building, and the heads of three women turned to look at their new arrival. No time. He bounded passed them, round the ovens and over the counter into the main café. Ah! He knew where he was. He'd eaten in here on one of his first dates with Rachel–

Trying to avoid distracting himself and ignoring the shouts behind him, Adam shoved the sack under a vacant table. It was unlikely he would see it again but it was better than being spotted with it – he would come back and try to collect it later.

He ran through the café entrance and into town. Brilliant! There were lots of people *and* he knew where he was. He was going to get away! With the knowledge of his location acting as the optimistic leg-up he needed, a plan began to fall into place as he started casually walking through town.

He checked over his shoulder. No one had followed him from the café. The helicopter was still roughly where it had been before, but the men would have touched ground by now. He accelerated into a sufficiently inconspicuous power-walk towards McDonalds. The plan was simple: he'd lock himself in the disabled toilet and relax until he had the strength to jump through the mirror.

Another look over his shoulder saw the end of this optimism. Three men dressed in black leather catsuits were also leaving the café. They were striding into the middle of town and looking in all directions, and people were giving them serious room.

Painfully, Adam slowed down to a walking pace, hoping that meant they'd be less likely to see him. Eventually, without any backward glancing, he reached McDonalds and walked through the door, across the restaurant and to the toilet corridor in the corner. Had they seen him? Had they followed him in? His heart was pounding and adrenaline rushed through his system... it'd take him several minutes to build his strength back. Did he have that much time?

His heart sank as he saw the red marker above the door handle that meant it was locked. Never in his experience of using McDonalds to get changed had a disabled person been using the toilet. God didn't like him today.

"Hurry up!" he shouted with as much conviction as he could, banging on the door. As he did so, a guy in a McDonald's uniform appeared from the '*Staff Only*' door at the other end of the corridor, giving him a funny look as he heard his shouts. He looked slightly younger than Adam and of a similar build, and he had "opportunity" written all over his face.

"In here," Adam said, grabbing the startled lad by the collar and pushing him into the guy's toilets.

"What are y– get the **** off me!"

There was no one in there.

"I don't want to hurt you mate," he said, pushing the guy against the wall inside.

"What *do* you want?" the guy asked.

"I... need you to take off your clothes," Adam said.

Obviously this was not what the guy had been hoping to hear. He took a swing at Adam, who ducked and punched him hard in the stomach. He fell to the floor, banging his head on the wall. Then he was still.

He was still breathing (thank God), but this was not good: robbery and assault, in the space of fifteen minutes. If he didn't escape now, he'd be inside for years.

A minute later, he walked out into the corridor wearing the McDonalds uniform... to meet three men dressed all in black.

They'd followed him.

Adam couldn't help but look startled. They didn't seem to take any notice, the first two saw what he was wearing and pushed passed him, muttering about checking the toilets. The other one stayed outside, apparently feeling his assistance in such a small task would be a waste of everyone's time.

202

An old man with crutches appeared from inside the disabled toilet, and, knowing he only had seconds, Adam pushed his way passed the man inside the toilet, locked the door and pulled on it to make sure it was secure. To his right: a beautiful mirror. The escape route. He stared at his reflection as hard as he could, but all he could see was his pumping chest and the sweat on his forehead. He was too tired to jump – he had to calm his body down.

After splashing water on his face, Adam sat on the toilet lid and breathed in for five seconds, then out for five. He felt like he was at primary school, lying down in the assembly hall listening to the sounds of the waves crashing against the shore from the relaxation CD. He tried to imagine them now, the slapping of the water as it curled into itself, the foaming of the surf as it was pulled backwards and forwards…

"He's been here! He's taken a worker's clothes!"

The sounds from outside shattered his pastoral vision.

"He's in there!"

A hammering erupted on the door. In the

corner of his eye, Adam could see it shake slightly under the pressure, but he tried to block it out. Seagulls were flying overhead, the sunlight glimmering from the water. More hammering. Two bikini-clad girls splashed water at each other, a yacht sailing peacefully behind them…

"Get the dynamite!"

On this announcement, Adam sat up. He gripped the edges of the sink and glared into the mirror, forcefully continuing the "steady" breathing. He imagined his feet leaving the ground as he was pulled into the glass. Yes. He could imagine it. This was normal. He'd done this lots of times now. It wasn't hard. He could feel himself start to slip away…

The explosion knocked him clean off his feet. The toilet door was blown all around him and he flew into the wall, cracking his head.

He had been so close.

One of the men rushed in, and bent his arms behind his back, causing him to cry out in pain. The other two were by his side in a flash, running through the smoke and rubble.

"Can I hear my rights?" he asked with false

confidence.

"Mutates don't have rights," the guy holding his arms said. He pulled him into a standing position and pushed him against the wall so his face was squashed against a tile. The blood he had lost when the door exploded was squeezed down his face.

Adam could see in his left eye one of the other two men come up to him, holding something the size of a television remote. A second later, he was released and something came into contact with his left arm, sending a surging pain through his whole body. He fell to the floor, numb.

He tried to get up, but couldn't move, just twitching pathetically. All he could do was watch as the men carried him out of the toilets and through McDonalds, generating many shocked gasps and expressions. But nobody got up to help.

Once they got outside, he was placed in the middle of the street, facing up at the cloudless sky. There were more gasps and shouts from the people around him. But still no one came to his rescue.

"We've got him," one of the men said, presumably into a walkie talkie. "Bring us in."

The world was cast in shadow as the menacing hulk of a helicopter appeared, blocking out the light from the sun as it descended towards them. As it did so, Adam could feel his eyes closing as the numbness started to consume him. He could just about see a large platform being lowered on ropes from the helicopter, touching the ground next to them before he was lifted onto it.

The last thing he felt was the whole thing being lifted from the ground, leaving the town and any chance of freedom behind.

*

"Try it on me," Philippa said.

"What?"

"Go on. Try and impose a thought on me. Think of like an image or something and try to get me to see it."

"You're mad."

"Just try it."

Evie stared at her sister's head with conviction. She focussed on her own forehead as much as she could, feeling wrinkles form across it as she strained her brain. She hadn't thought of an image yet, first focussing on... "projecting".

Then Philippa's hair turned blonde and her face turned into Evie's, which suddenly looked shocked. But she could also see Philippa, with her naturally brown hair. She was seeing the two images at once, not next to each other like a screen when two people play Xbox together, but almost like she had another pair of eyes and another brain so she could take in two images at the same time, completely exclusive to each other.

"Philly..."

"Have you thought of an image yet?"

"Philly, I can see..."

"Come on," Philippa said, getting up from the bed and starting to walk round the room. "Try and get me to see something."

As Philippa moved, Evie could no longer see herself sat on the bed. Instead, the image changed into a sweeping view of her own bedroom, even though she kept her own head motionless.

And then something clicked in her mind and she understood what she was seeing.

"Philly... I think I'm... in your head."

Philippa turned and Evie could see herself staring up worriedly, whilst simultaneously seeing her sister looking down confusedly at her.

"What do you mean?"

"I... can see everything you're seeing."

"...I don't believe you."

"G... go out of the room and do something. I'll try and tell you what you did."

Without another word, Philippa left the room and closed the door. She went across the landing and into their parents' room. As she did so, the image of what Philippa could see became more blurry to Evie. She tried to focus hard to retain the image.

Philippa looked around the room for inspiration. She didn't know what to do – this was ludicrous. Unable to think of anything else, she grabbed the corner of their parents' duvet and pulled it back so that the corner was peeled halfway down the bed. She left the room and went back to where Evie was sat on the bed.

"You pulled Mum and Dad's covers back a bit," Evie said simply.

Philippa opened her mouth but did not speak – she was stunned.

"I can see you now as you're stood there. But I can also see myself through *your* eyes. It's like I can see two things at once."

Philippa sat next to her on the bed, still speechless.

"I could feel it getting fainter as you went into their room. I had to concentrate harder."

"Make me do something," Philippa said, finding her vocal chords again.

"What?"

"If you can get inside my brain, you might be able to control what I'm doing."

"Can I hell, I–"

"You won't know until you try."

"But I don't w–"

"You're my sister. I don't mind. Just give it a go – what harm can it do?

Evie focussed on the image that was not coming from her eyes and tried to block out what she was actually seeing herself. As she did, she could almost feel herself falling into her sister's body, growing slightly taller, her chest growing slightly bigger, her hair shortening.

"Philly?" she said.

"Yeah?" she felt herself say.

She didn't reply, and instead, tried to move Philippa's body. She brought her left foot forward and back down onto the floor. She felt a little wobbly, like she was drunk, but she had definitely done that herself. She turned round and walked out of the room and into the bathroom, leaving herself on the bed.

She saw a glass on the window ledge which their dad often had a whisky out of when he was in the bath. She carefully gripped her alien fingers around the sides, picking it up. She brought it to the sink, ran the tap and filled it with water. She brought it to her lips and tried to drink it, but her shaking hand missed and spilt it down her top.

The cold water against her skin shocked her into leaving Philippa's mind, and the only image she could see was Philippa walking back into the bedroom with a damp patch on her purple top.

"That was amazing!" Evie exclaimed.

"Did... did you make me do that?" Philippa asked confusedly, sitting down next to Evie on the bed and pulling the wet patch away from her skin.

"Yes! Why, what did it feel like for you?"

"Like... like I did that of my own accord. I went into the bathroom and had a drink... because I just did. Because I wanted to, I guess. I felt a little bit shaky, but if you hadn't said, I'd have thought that I'd done that myself..."

Evie and Philippa stared at each other in amazement. This was incredible. She'd gone from simple mental projection to complete mind control in the space of two minutes.

"There's so many possibilities here Eve," Philippa said slowly. "The scale of this is incredible... we don't even *know* what else you can do. But you've got to keep quiet about it. We don't want—"

Evie's ringtone erupted from her phone. She looked at the screen to see who was calling.

Oh God...

"Hi Rosie," she said, trying to sound as casual as possible.

"Evie, I need to speak to you."

"Fire away!"

"In person."

"Oh, I'm afraid I'm a little tied up at the moment."

"If you don't come over right now, I'll tell everyone you're a mutate."

As soon she put the phone down, Evie left the house and walked towards Rosie's, feeling sick. They were best friends – surely she'd understand that she'd not done it on purpose...?

The sun had gone in now, so when she turned the corner onto Rosie's street, she didn't see her at first sat on a low brick wall in the darkness. She did a double take at her silhouette and saw her friend's solemn face in shadow.

"Hi Rosie."

"Mark told me what happened today. About what you made him do."

"Look, I didn't do it on purpose, I swear. I didn't know before then that I could... do that."

"Do what? What exactly do *you* call being a freak?" Rosie spat.

"...Are you serious?"

"Damn ****ing right I'm serious. How long have you been keeping this covered up? Why didn't you tell me, your supposed *best friend*, that you were one of these... mutates everyone keeps talking about?"

"I didn't kn–"

"You didn't tell me because you thought you'd use your freaky little ****ing power to try and seduce Mark behind my back."

"No I di–"

"Don't deny it. You've always wanted him. I remember you saying so before I started seeing him. Every time you see us together I can see how jealous you are."

These sentences hurt more than anything Evie had ever had to deal with before. Probably because somewhere, there was some truth in what was being said.

"Why can't you just be happy for me?" Rosie continued. "We're supposed to be best friends!"

"BUT I DIDN'T MEAN FOR IT TO HAPPEN!" she screamed, desperate to understand why her friend was being so irrational. As she did, Evie felt herself split. Before she'd even finished her outburst, she had started viewing the argument from behind Rosie's eyes too. It did not disconcert her as much this time, and she was able to finish off

213

her exclamation without confusing herself.

"Course you ****ing did! You've fancied him longer than I have!" she felt herself shout. As she did so, she saw someone running through a garden behind her own body in the darkness.

Evie turned round to see who was behind her, but before she could see anything, something collided with her, sending her flying, and held her into the ground.

"AH! ROSIE... HELP ME!"

Seeing only the tarmac of the road through her own eyes, Evie felt herself being pushed into the floor by what she/Rosie could see to be a muscular figure dressed from head to foot in black. Another stepped out from the shadows and walked towards Rosie, who was stood paralysed by the wall.

"You didn't see anything," the man said to her. "Did you?"

Evie felt her head shake, a fear that was not her own welling inside her.

"Now go," he said.

There was barely a hesitation, and Evie felt Rosie turn and run away until she was ripped from Evie's perspective, and all she could see was the road again, pressed into her face by her assailant.

She heard the other man's footsteps as he walked back towards them.

"Please–" she started to say, but felt a strong shock in her left side before the world was consumed by darkness.

*

Adam's eyes started to open. His head was throbbing. He could feel cold metal underneath him, and there was a steady beeping noise coming from above his head to the right. He tried to move his arms to rub his eyes, but felt something on his wrists holding them down by his sides.

He blinked repeatedly until his surroundings came into view and craned his neck to try to work out where he was. The room was quite large, with grey matted walls. There were lots of screens facing away from him on top of boxes with lots of flashing lights, buttons and dials. A fat bald man in a white coat was the only other person in the room, leaning on one of the machines and typing into a computer.

Adam was lying in his underwear (and a bandage round the top of his head) on something which could not be described as a bed because it seemed to be made of steel and had no pillow. What it did have was a number of wires that protruded from its base, presumably connected somehow to the machines, which snaked into various orifices of his body, some of which were there before and some which weren't. Two tubes that curled up into his nose made him feel like he had just been in a car accident, but a very thin wire poking into a new, small hole at the base of his neck confirmed he was not in intensive care. Metal rings strapped both legs and both arms to the slab on which he lay, making it impossible for him to get up.

The man turned round and Adam slammed his eyes shut.

"I know you're awake," a low voice spoke. "I've been monitoring your brain activity. Not that there's an awful lot going on in there – trying to rob a bank the *day* after we announce mutates to be real... madness..."

Adam opened his eyes and saw the man

standing near him, adjusting switches on a large machine without looking at him. He had several large moles and two parallel chins from the non-flattering angle which Adam could see him from.

"*We*? So you're the government then?"

"If you like."

Adam watched as the man moved to the other side of the "bed," twisting what could have been a volume control on a CD player had there not been copious menacing wires protruding from the front and disappearing from view.

"So what am I doing here Doctor Frankenstein?"

Adam was surprised to hear him give an answer:

"You, are the subject of a very complicated experiment Mr Brookes," the man said, almost politely. "A very *successful* experiment might I add, resulting in," (he began to talk in a steady, rhythmic pattern, as if reciting something he had read countless times before) "an ability to teleport yourself and anything in direct contact with your skin, from one reflective surface, simply by looking at yourself in it, to another within a half mile radius. As of yet, you are unable to pinpoint exactly where you will reappear, and the movement often results in a high level of fatigue for several minutes." (He started speaking normally again): "You may have noticed there are absolutely no reflective surfaces in this laboratory, Mr Brookes. We're prepared for you."

A quick look around confirmed what he had said – there was no escape route. The restraints seemed to tighten around Adam's limbs even harder.

"Wow. You know my name *and* what I can do. You worked a lot out from sticking a few wires up my ass."

The man laughed slightly. "Oh no, Mr Brookes. We've been analysing your progress for quite some time. These 'wires' are merely there to monitor all essential bodily functions, to check you're not going to die on us."

"I'm flattered you care so much about me," the sarcasm appeared in Adam's mouth from nowhere. "But preserving my life didn't seem too high on your agenda when you were blowing half of town apart to test your stun guns on me."

The man laughed again. Clearly he wasn't used to people resorting to humour when their fate was uncertain. "Right you are, Mr Brookes, quite right you are. What I mean is, we want to make sure you don't die on us so that we can go onto the next phase."

"What's the next phase?" Adam asked, realising that (worryingly), the man had no qualms in telling him anything he wanted to know.

"Cultivation. To take what, at the moment, is making you unique, and mass produce it."

"...Why? Surely if everyone had my powers, terrorism would be worse than it's ever been."

"Right again Mr Brookes, which is why we're *not* planning on giving it to everyone. Terrorism is exactly what we want to avoid. The powers will be distributed to the United States Army, and America will go from being the greatest superpower on Earth to the *only* superpower on Earth. Those idiots in the Middle East won't dare lift a finger when they learn of our biologically superior manpower..."

Adam could hear the jubilation and pride in his voice. It was clear he'd been waiting to explain this controversial government plot for a while, and that he had had a big hand in it. More worrying however, was the pressing fact that he had absolutely no reservation in telling Adam everything he wanted to know...

"So..." Adam tried to voice his concerns. "What do you plan on doing with me once you've stolen my biological superior...*ness*?"

"*Stolen*?" The scientist sounded perplexed. "How can we steal something that we gave to you in the first place?"

"...What do you mean?"

"You didn't *really* think it was nature did you? That God decided you were special and made you part of the... next wave of humans? The mutated gene is not *mutated* at all. It was *invented* – created from scratch by a team of brilliant scientists," (Adam couldn't help wonder if he was referring partly to himself here) "and inserted into the DNA of people across America without their knowledge to test its effectiveness. Of course, it's been trial and error, and many have been unsuccessful, but recently there have been some breakthroughs. You are one of the first people the crafted gene has had a positive effect on. One of our success stories. I hope feel as honoured as you should do."

Adam didn't know what to say. He felt sick. He had thought he was special, that, as stupid as it sounded, maybe God *had* chosen him over the others. But in reality, he'd been nothing but an unknowing guinea pig in a political science experiment that there was now no escaping from.

"As for your question Mr Brookes – what *are* we going to do with you?" the scientist leaned over Adam to look at him properly for the first time. "Once we've taken the data we need to transfer the teleporting ability to our soldiers, there won't be much point hanging onto you. You don't look like you'd do particularly well in the army," he said, tauntingly squeezing on Adam's bare bicep "and if we let you go, you'd only try and rob another bank. Not to mention tell people all the highly confidential information I've just told you.

"No..." he said, bringing his face close to Adam's so that their noses were almost touching and Adam could feel the man's saliva spraying on his chin as he spoke. "In a few minutes, when I've taken the last few readings, we're going to kill you. Another electric shock probably, but one that you won't wake up from this time, with your pathetic excuse for quick wittedness and attempted rebellion..."

Adam could see his own terrified reflection in the man's deep brown eyes as his imminent death became apparent.

"Your body will join those of the other successful mutates, and be destroyed in one of our furnaces – never to be seen or heard from again."

His own terrified reflection.

"You're such a sweet talker," Adam said. "Mind if I try?"

The scientist looked down at him confusedly.

"Ok, here goes: You really do have the most beautiful eyes."

"Wha – NOOO!" the man screamed, as

Adam shot up towards his pupils, leaving nothing but an empty metal slab in the middle of the laboratory.

*

"What exactly do *you* call being a freak?"

Rosie, a hundred times bigger than she usually was, picked her up with one hand above the town. The houses looked like dots from where Evie was, high in the air, the wind blowing her hair around her face in all directions.

"You thought you'd use your freakish little power to try and seduce Mark behind my back!" Rosie's huge head said, and Evie felt her ribs begin to snap in her friend's hand. She was being crushed by her huge fingers... she could feel herself start to black out...

Evie opened her eyes with a gasp, relief from waking up quickly disappearing when she remembered what had happened. She shivered. She was only wearing underwear, but was sure that the shivers were not from the cold. She was strapped to a metal slab, and a number of wires were coiling into different parts of her body.

She looked around the large room. As far as

she could tell, she was alone, but was surrounded by a number of flashing screens and machines, presumably taking readings from the wires that were inside her. As she stared at one of the screens to try and make out what it said, a young man appeared from its centre, emerging from it as if it were made of water, and she decided she must still be dreaming.

He fell onto the floor and lost his footing, picking himself up quickly. He too was only wearing underwear and had wires hanging out of him, which he hastily began to pull out as he looked around urgently.

"Who are you?" he said as soon as he saw her, continuing to scan the room for any other sign of life. "What's your power?" he asked, as if deciding his first question wasn't important enough.

"Wh... er... I don't really know. Mental powers? Mind control?"

He looked at her to see if she was joking. Apparently her panic stricken face said otherwise.

"Brilliant. We'll be able to get out of here."

"But like... I've only ever made my sister

spill a glass of water on herself."

He looked at her in the same way before rolling his eyes.

"...But I've only known about my powers like a day!"

"So lame..." he muttered under his breath as he walked towards her, pulling at the shackles which held her down, trying to work out how to open them.

"Lame?? Why, what can you do?"

He looked at her again.

"...Didn't you see me pop out of that screen?"

"Well, yes, but..."

"I can teleport using reflective surfaces."

"Oh... cool."

He finished his circle of her, and stalked over to one of the computers.

"Any idea how to get you out?" he asked, studying the screen and moving the mouse to try and find something.

"Er... not r–"

A loud siren started buzzing and a red light whirled in the corner of the room. It was probably loud enough to be heard throughout the whole building, although of course he didn't know how big the building was.

"Shit! Is that because you touched the computer??"

"Er... I don't think so..." he said, panic evident in his face. "They know that I've escaped so they're probably looking for me."

"Shit!" Evie said. "What are you gonna d–"

"Ah!" he said, pressing a button Evie couldn't see. The bottom of the slab she lay on opened up, and another keyboard rose on a pole from inside, facing away from her. He dashed over to her and studied the keyboard, before pressing something which made the shackles open up.

"Thanks!" she said under the siren, standing up and pulling the wires from herself.

"No problem."

"So... are you gonna teleport us now? Can you do two people?"

"Well, I would... but my body gets tired after each time. I'll have to wait a few minutes for my heart rate to go back to normal."

"Are you serious??" she said, staring at the door to the room. "They're *looking* for you!"

"It's alright. It's probably a big place, so it'll take them age–"

Before Adam could finish his sentence, another man in a white coat burst into the room and screamed back out into the corridor "I'VE GOT HIM! HE'S IN HERE!"

"COME ON!" Adam yelled to Evie, sprinting towards the door. He knocked the man clean off his feet as he left and Evie, terrified, followed him through the door.

They were in a large corridor, and two men at the other end were sprinting in their direction. Adam quickly opened another door on their right and they found themselves in a small dressing room, full of clothes on hangers. Apparently this was where they changed from normal people into mad scientists.

"Teleport!" Evie told him.

"I can't!" Adam said, remembering what had happened in McDonalds. "It'll take me ages to get my heart rate down and they're right behind us!"

"And you said I was lame…"

He grabbed the side of a large table and after he indicated, she did the same. They heaved it in front of the door to stop anyone following them in. The sirens continued to blare as Adam had a look through the large window which stretched across the back wall. It was dark outside, but he could see they were three storeys high. A drainpipe passed their window and went all the way to the ground. Their route to freedom.

Adam grabbed a hat stand from next to the wall and rammed it into the window. It didn't shatter, but created a substantial hole. He kicked around the hole, knocking more glass through until it was big enough for them to fit.

"Help me!" he snapped at Evie, grabbing clothes off hangers and putting them round the smashed glass.

"No way am I jumping out of there! We're three storeys up!"

Adam carefully lifted himself through, putting his feet on the window ledge. He grabbed the drainpipe next to him firmly with both hands, turning himself around.

"Fine," he said. "Stay here and get pulled apart by the loony brigade. I'm out of here."

He began to pull himself down the

drainpipe, bouncing his feet off the wall and gripping the rest of his body tightly onto it.

A heavy banging erupted on the door behind Evie, and she saw the table start to move. She quickly squeezed through the hole in the window, across the ledge, and followed Adam down the drainpipe.

"That was quick!" Adam said, looking up to see a face full of pink fabric. "Nice ass!"

"I've known you five minutes and I already hate you!" she shouted over the siren. "We're gonna get killed and you don't seem to give a fAHHHHHHHHHH!"

The drainpipe came loose from the top of the building under their weight and they felt themselves falling backwards as the pipe swung at an angle until it was parallel with the ground. It remained jutted out from the building, but Adam could feel it slipping through his fingers and heard the groaning sound as their weight threatened to snap it off completely.

"We've gotta let go!" he said.

They were still at least two storeys high.

"No way!" Evie shouted back, her arms and legs wrapped tightly around the drainpipe.

"It'll completely come off otherwise!"

Adam closed his eyes, let go and dropped to the floor. His feet hit the hard concrete and a pain shot up his leg as they did so – he had fallen from a significant height. He ran underneath Evie, who was dangling by her arms, and slipping fast.

"I'm underneath you!" he shouted. "Let go!"

"No!"

"LET GO YOU IDIOT!"

She let go, screaming as she went. Adam managed to soften her blow, but they collided with each other and then the ground, water from a large puddle covering their bare skin.

"Terrific."

They stood up and ran around the side of the building, staying close to the stone wall. It was a huge complex, in the middle of what looked like a large square holding facility. There was an empty yard all around the building, up to a tall mesh fence with barbed wire snaked at the top in ominous loops. All Adam could see outside the fence in the dark were tall thin trees.

A bright spotlight burst from above,

dazzling them both. They started to run away from the building, unsure exactly where they were going.

The ground was pounded at their feet by something as they ran – gunfire. Warning shots?

Adam looked around him, unsure of where to run, what to do. As he did, he saw more men wearing black catsuits run out of the building towards them, guns in their hands. He grabbed Evie's hand and ran in the opposite direction, only for more men to appear from that side of the facility. They were all holding guns.

Adam pivoted on his heel, looking around for any chance of escape, but there was none. The men were getting closer, about twenty metres away now, spreading out into a circle around the two of them. He had not forgotten what the scientist had said before he'd escaped: *"there won't be much point hanging onto you."* They were going to be slaughtered.

He raised his hands in the air as the guns were pointed at them. Evie did the same. They were back to back, facing outwards at the constantly encroaching army of about thirty men, each one with a lethal weapon in their hand.

"Do your mind control," Adam said under his breath. "Make them not kill us."

"I can't. I've never–"

"Well don't you think now would be a good time to try it?"

A distorted voice echoed from a microphone somewhere:

"Make no sudden moves. We have you completely surrounded."

"Yeah, no shit," Adam muttered.

Evie looked in terror at the men around her. Her body was completely shaking and she felt like she was going to faint. She slowly turned her head to see how many of them there were, desperate to make them leave her alone...

And what she had hoped for but never expected to happen, happened. She was in a circle around herself, viewing her trembling body from 360° in a surreal, simultaneous image. She could feel the minds of all the men she was inside, pushing back at her. Her head was starting to hurt already from being split across so many different people.

But she knew what she had to do. Slowly,

she turned around and watched as all the men did exactly that all around her – turning to face away from the two of them.

"Omigod..." Adam whispered. "Did you–"

"Yes!" she shouted, starting to feel her mind buckle under the strain. "But I can't hold them like that much longer! You've got to get us out of here!"

Adam knew that was impossible. His heart was racing so much that it would take a joint and a nice long massage to calm him down enough to teleport the two of them out of there.

"I can't. I'm too worked up!"

"THEN GET UN-WORKED UP!" Evie screamed, her hands clutching her head as she started to go dizzy. "OR WE'RE GOING TO DIE!"

The spotlight glimmered off the back of one of the men's metal belts. Adam ran tentatively over to him and looked into the shiny surface. He had to do it.

Evie could feel all the men fighting back, trying to turn round. She was holding them all individually in place, a mental arm wrestle that she could only keep going for so long.

Adam pressed his face close to the belt, but as he did so, he knew for sure that it wasn't going to work. He could feel no link between himself and the metal and he couldn't see his reflection very well. His pumping heart was not going to let them make a jump. He heard Evie scream and turned to look at her. She was curled up on the floor now, her hands clenched in her hair.

"HURRY!" she screamed, one leg flailing to the side as her control slowly slipped.

"I can't do it..." They were going to die. Why should they die? They were the only innocent ones here. It should be the others. The men should–

"MAKE THEM SHOOT EACH OTHER!" he yelled.

"WHAT??"

"MAKE THEM ALL SHOOT THE ONE NEXT TO THEM!"

Evie fought her way to the forefront of their collective brainpower. She could feel the weapons in her hand, and forced her arm up so that the guns were all pointed to the man to her right. Adam watched as the circle around him did this in unison like a kaleidoscope, all aiming to kill their nearest partner.

Evie felt her finger on the triggers... It felt so wrong.

"I CAN'T! I CAN'T KILL THESE PEOPLE!"

"IF YOU DON'T, WE'RE GOING TO DIE!"

He was right.

She screamed and pulled back on the triggers.

Adam dived to the ground as what sounded like one incredibly loud gunshot cracked through the night air. The men all dropped to the floor, destroying the human wall that had surrounded the two of them.

Adam ran over to Evie who was motionless on the floor – had she been shot? Her eyes were closed, but she was breathing – she had passed out.

He saw a movement to his right in the light – one of the men was attempting to get up. He ran over and kicked him in the jaw. The man yelled and went flying back onto the floor, moaning. Adam looked at his catsuit – he had been shot in the side, and although bleeding heavily, would survive. Perfect.

Adam snatched his gun up from next to him and shoved it against his wheezing face.

"Tell me how to get out of here," he said. "Or you go the same way as the rest of these men."

The man looked up into Adam's eyes with unmistakable terror. Then he reached into his pocket (to which Adam pushed the gun even further into his face), took out a small keypad, pointed it behind them and pressed a button on it.

Through the darkness, Adam could see some of the fencing part to create a man-sized exit. Their door to freedom.

He looked down at the man who had just saved his life. He had only done it because he knew he would have been killed otherwise. He would have killed *them* if he'd had the chance. It was these thoughts that Adam pushed to the forefront of his mind when he pulled back on the trigger and the man's heavy breathing ceased.

He ran over to Evie, and keeping the gun in one hand, picked her up in his arms. He was holding the gun so awkwardly that he knew if anyone confronted him he wouldn't be able to aim properly, but he felt better for having it. He looked over his shoulder at the empty complex and sprinted out of the new exit before anyone else could leave the building and attack them.

He was now in what could only be described as a forest. Adam was grateful for the trees he weaved between as he ran, knowing they would make him much harder to follow. Building the complex in a forest was no doubt intentional to keep it from being discovered, but it must have been a nightmare for them to get to and from.

After five minutes, his run had steadied to a jog. A stitch had broken out in his side to remind him of how unfit he was, and the girl he carried grew heavier by the second. He slowed even further to a walk, and eventually stopped when he reached a gently flowing river.

Looking behind him again to check no one had caught up with them, he laid her on the floor and ran down the river bank to get some water. He ran back up with his hands cupped, and dripped it slowly onto her forehead.

As she stirred, he held her shoulder and

shook her gently until her eyes opened and she screamed.

"Shhhh!"

"W– where are we?"

"We've escaped. You did it."

"...I killed them?"

"All but one. But I got him."

She looked away from him with an emotionless face, unsure what to decide how she felt about what she had done; she had saved their lives, but at what cost?

"I'm Adam," he said, holding out his hand.

She sat up, and eventually took it.

"Evie."

"...That was incredible what you did back there."

"Killing a load of people? Yeah – amazing."

"Those men were evil. They would have killed us if you hadn't beat them to it."

"How do you know?"

"Before I escaped, one of their scientists was talking to me. He told me that we're all part of a big government experiment. They *made* us like this. All so they can test out which powers work then they can make an army of people like us. Then they were going to kill us. *Our government* were going to kill us."

Evie looked at the ground and shivered. She wrapped her arms round her legs, and thought about what she had just been told.

"I don't believe you," she said quietly.

"What?"

"I said I don't believe you. You can't tell me that our government wanted to kill us. Our entire government is not made up of... evil men. This might be a splinter group or something, but not everyone. I... I just don't believe that. I can't believe that."

"But the President–"

"Maybe the President was just saying what he *thought* was true. Maybe he's being influenced. Maybe not. But it can't be *everyone*. It would have gotten out."

"It won't be everyone; just the people at the top."

"Not all the top men in our country are evil! They couldn't have all gotten to the position they're in by being nasty, selfish men."

The words echoed around in her head, and she tried to find enough truth in them to believe what she had said. It was easier said than done.

"Regardless, whoever they are, we need to take them down."

"...What?"

"We know where their base is. We know what they're doing. We've escaped, and it's up to us to stop it. There could be hundreds more people in there like us who've been experimented on, and we need to stop them being killed."

Evie laughed at the ludicrous words the boy in front of her was saying.

"You just said you thought the *whole* government was behind this."

"...And?"

"*And*, you can't take the whole United States government down."

"Why not?"

"Er... because you're just a kid?" she said, deciding he was insane.

"Actually, I'm nineteen, but that's irrelevant. We're not just kids. We've been made special. So special in fact, that you were able to kill about thirty of them in the space of a second. They've created a bigger problem than they had

240

to start with... they'll be taken down by their own creations."

"You're mad."

He looked to his right at the river and wondered if she was right. But did it matter? He couldn't see any other logical next step now. They knew who he was – he couldn't escape them forever. He had to confront this problem head on, and if it killed him, it killed him. But he wasn't going to just give up. He had to try and help anyone else who was not in a position to fight for themselves.

Then a dangerously familiar whirring noise caught his attention. It was from the direction of the complex, getting louder. Adam looked at the way they had come from and saw a green light pierce through the trees from above.

And they were running again, parallel to the river, trying to escape those in their pursuit. If they were found, they would be killed where they stood.

They reached a stone bridge that ran over the river, and Adam pulled Evie onto it before crouching down so that they were hidden by its sides. He put his hands on either side of her to make sure she was still, hoping that they would go unnoticed.

The whirring of propellers grew louder and louder, and he desperately tried to think of a plan should the helicopter fly directly overhead and see them.

"Try and get inside their heads," he said.

"But I can't even see them!"

"Just try!"

Terrified, Evie peered over the edge of the bridge and saw the helicopter in the sky. She imagined someone inside, controlling it, pictured his eye searching for the two of them... and she was inside his head. She could feel his desperation as he scoured the darkness for any sign of movement. Evie could see the bridge through his eyes and saw her head peeking over the side. She bobbed down quickly so that she could not be seen, but the sudden movement caught the attention of the man whose eyes she was looking through.

"They've seen us."

"*Shit*!"

Evie felt herself press a button on the control unit. She peered over the bridge again and watched in horror as what looked like a rocket launcher descended from the bottom of the helicopter.

"They're going to fire!"

On a screen in front of her, she saw a cross on a set of telescopic sights. The man adjusted a joystick so that the bridge was in the centre and the lines crossed over exactly where she was crouched. She tried to pull the joystick in another direction, but could feel the strain of the distance between them as her hand moved to another part of the dashboard. She could not control what he was doing.

"Come on!" Adam yelled, jumping up onto the side of the bridge, facing away from the sights.

Evie saw the green light from the helicopter reflect off the water and realised what Adam's plan was. She pulled away from the man so she could only see through her own eyes as she followed Adam onto the side of the bridge, in plain sight of the targeted weapon.

"Go!" she screamed, climbing onto his back and wrapping her arms and legs tightly around his torso – he was her only escape. He jumped off the bridge and fell downwards towards the river.

She heard the explosion of the rocket being fired behind her head and felt its searing heat before they were pulled into the water...

The Return

Robert's hand rapped tentatively on the large oak door. Through the aging wood he heard the echo bounce off the walls in the utility room, like a fairy trapped in a jar. When he had lived there twenty five years ago there hadn't been a doorbell and he supposed there never would be – it wouldn't be right.

Robert had been toying with the idea of going back to his childhood home ever since he had left at the age of eleven, when his father had decided that he'd had "enough of this madness." Up to now he'd never found the courage to return, worried what he may or may not find. However he'd recently been forced to reconsider after a callous change of pace:

For weeks, they had known that something was not right with their son William; constantly tired, unable to shake off a cold and bruising at the slightest bump. They had taken him to the doctors and one routine blood test later, they were told he had acute lymphoblastic

245

leukaemia. No steady build up. No warning. Just a firm diagnosis with the guarantee that the doctors would do everything they could over the following months.

William, an eight-year-old animal enthusiast, already knew how serious the implications of this could be. When they had told him in the softest way possible what was happening, his bubbly personality had shifted instantly. He went from being a conversationalist to someone who only really spoke when asked a question. His high speed car chases around the house had turned into him pushing a lorry back and forth on the windowsill. Worst of all, he had stopped their regular update of what he wanted to be in the future, a topic which had always been one of his favourites, whether it was pop star, zoo keeper or astronaut week.

Robert knew William was being so distant because the reality of his condition was all he could think about. He had never been able to let something go once it was in his head, but there had never been anything even remotely this big before. He needed something else to focus his thoughts on. Something so wonderfully awe-inspiring that it would fill his days and dreams, and his medical dilemma would become a minor complication in the vast tapestry of life.

Robert was so deep in thought that he was startled when a woman, who was advanced in years and beyond grey, opened the door and he was hit with a pungent odour of lavender perfume.

"Can I help you?" she asked.

Beneath the copious wrinkles was the face of a kind lady. Her welcoming smile put him under a spell and drew him into the house, to the extent that he almost forgot to answer her question. He restrained himself however and replied "I'm Robert Baker. I've come to see the house. We spoke–"

"–On the phone," she concluded for him, her voice brimming with understanding, reminding him somewhat of his mother. "I'm sure it holds many wonderful memories for you Mr Baker."

"I hope so," he muttered to himself.

She stepped to one side, allowing him entry into his old home. He wiped his shoes on the mat, resisting the unmistakable urge to take them off and hurl them into the corner of the room as he did when he was a child. As William had done only weeks ago. Robert knew this urge should not still have been there, but it was; was everything else? He walked through the utility room, into the living room and looked around for the answer to his question.

The walls had diminished from their once vibrant orange to a dusky peach, and the room was significantly smaller than he remembered it. It didn't mean the house was any less magical did it?

"Feel free to explore where you want to," the woman said, walking slowly towards where the kitchen used to be. "Let me know if you need anything."

"I'll be having a look round the garden, if that's ok?" Robert called after her.

"Goes without saying, doesn't it dear?"

His heart skipped a beat – did she know what he'd come to see?

Robert had decided beforehand that he was not going to sprint wildly into the garden. He had to do this in a calm and composed manner, otherwise, what he found might be too great a shock for him. Either way.

Taking a deep breath, he left the house through the back door and walked deliberately slowly along the grass, determined to keep himself under control. He walked parallel to the varnished wooden fence; ironically implying he needed a guide to the place he had escaped to countless times. He passed the pond which reflected the glistening sun, and blissful memories of gliding across the water flickered through his mind, the tips of his toes his only body part getting wet. It brought forward a more recent memory too, still years ago, but one that for some reason was etched into his brain like it was yesterday: The first time they had taken William to feed the ducks. Even from the confines of his pram he had become instantly mesmerised with the animals, and Robert had had to run to the shop for more bread.

He wished he could run now. He clenched the insides of his pockets in repressed frustration – if it was a lifetime since he was last here, it was nothing compared to the length of time this single journey seemed to be taking him.

William's fascination with animals had only grown with age. Their annual trip to Chester Zoo in the summer was always talked about afterwards until around Christmas time, then anticipated again until the following summer. Like his future jobs though, this was not something he had mentioned since the news...

Finally, Robert reached the end of the fence at the back of the garden and, just as he remembered, there was a raised varnished square at the bottom, on a hinge like a small door. He pulled it open and saw the perfectly round hole that it concealed. His heart rate accelerated – did this mean he hadn't imagined it? Why would this hole be here if not to lead to...?

Not caring about getting mud on his jeans, he dropped to his knees and began to feed himself through. He'd only had to duck back in the day, but now there was no other alternative than crawling. Upon emerging, he stood up and stared ahead at the narrow, snaking path.

Leaving his "keep-calm" mindset on the other side of the fence, Robert sprinted down the curved passage, thoughts flying frantically through his head. Although the hole in the fence suggested he had not imagined it, he still had no idea if they would be there. Surely it was impossible? Surely *they* were impossible? But what if they weren't? He could share them with his unwell son... he could pass on the magical childhood that he himself had had – everything would be ok!

The further along the path he ran, the less he registered where or who he was. All he was sure of was that at the end would be a glimmer of hope for a brighter future, or the biggest disappointment of his entire life.

As he neared the end he thought he could start to hear singing. Was *this* proof it was no fantasy? Yes! No. He couldn't believe; he *refused* to believe it until he could see them with his own eyes.

The sun emerged from behind a cloud and cast the world in a beautiful yellow light as Robert reached the end of the path and stepped into the circular enclosure. But it wasn't that which dazzled him. It wasn't that which created an immense warmth from the tips of his toes to the marrow of his bones. The music filled his heart as he gazed in wonder at their tiny, animate little bodies fluttering around his head, singing to their returned master in the illuminated dust.

Like a wonderfully warm medicine, the magic seeped inside him as realisation hit: the dream was real. He was complete again, and soon William would be too. Everything was beautiful, magical.

He was home.

Bridge Of Sighs

Why did I come here?

That's a stupid question. I came here for the same reason everyone comes to Oxford: to get a good degree to get a good job to get rich to get happy. Simple steps.

The steps... You'd never imagine from outside how ugly they are, a bright yellow band running across each one, denying them any integrity. You couldn't miss them unless you stared at the roof.

If I'm here for the same reason as everyone else, why do I feel so separated from them all? I was expecting them to just be toffs from Harrow and Eaton, but they're not all like that. That stereotype is unfair. It's just that everyone else here is "passionate" about their subject. So am *I* if you look at my personal statement, but I think deep down, I've always known that they were empty words.

Don't get me wrong, no one forced me into this. For the past few years it has been me alone who has been saying that I want to study English Literature. It was only *because* of this that my mum and teachers have encouraged and helped me to do the best I could, so I could go to the "best" possible university. I bullied my subconscious into submission. As usual, I've only myself to blame.

I reach the top of the steps.

Why have I allowed it to get to this? Eight weeks into a degree I hate, feeling like my life is essentially over. Yes, I like reading, but don't most people? That doesn't mean they should do an English degree. I'd sooner pick up a copy of Heat Magazine than anything by Shakespeare. That can't be a good sign.

I was in the English Faculty Library yesterday, surrounded by people poring over literally dozens of books at a time, and all I could think was "why?" Who cares what Blake or Chaucer meant? They were just single men (not women, notice) in history who had opinions and could write consistently. But we live in 2012; surely we should be writing new stories for the simple purpose of entertainment? If you want politics, flick Question Time on. If you want *sixteenth century* politics then yes, treat yourself and wipe the dust off your Shakespeare collection... but why would you?

And don't get me started on poetry. Which sick bastard invented the poem? And why did it catch on? If I said today I had a great idea for a new TV show where no one says what they mean (the temptation to revert back to Question Time is tenacious) and there are long, vague scenes in which people and places all represent something else entirely, I'd be picking the colour padding for my cell before I could say "to be or not to be" (the most ludicrously overused and overrated quotation I've ever had the misfortune to study). It wouldn't work on TV, and it doesn't work on paper either.

I remember expressing to Mr Jenkins, my A Level English teacher, this bewilderment over our obsession with poems and old literature:

"You want to be an author, right Beth?" was his initial response.

"Well, it's a possible career option, bu–"

"So yes. Have you ever heard then of the expression: Standing on the shoulders of giants?"

"It's one of Oasis's weaker albums," is *not* what I said. I'd heard him use this cliché before, so I had come prepared:

"Yes sir, but do you not think it's possible that if we spend so long admiring the giant's shoulder blades, we could become too obsessed and never climb higher?"

Personally, I was quite impressed with my extension of this flawed metaphor, but Mr Jenkins put down his tea and stared at me as if I had just claimed I was Shakespeare reincarnated, so I knew the conversation was over before it had really begun. It was then that I started to wonder if I was really cut out to be an English student.

I can see the Sheldonian Theatre through the window. From the outside, it looks great. But so does the bridge, and the yellow bands tell a different story once you're inside. Maybe the theatre does too, but I won't ever find out.

So if I don't like English, what do I like? Going shopping. Seeing my friends. Watching Scrubs. Going on Facebook. Texting boys... All standard stuff.

Why can't that be fine? Why *should* I be

pressured into having a "passion" for something perceived as academic? I'm still hardworking. All A's at GCSE and A Level. Surely that's enough to prove to a prospective employer I've got a good work ethic? Do I really need to waste three years of my life pretending I'm interested in something just to secure a "good job?" And even if I found one, would it be worth it? I'd have lost my youth to years of being crushed between titles and blurbs. To me, that's tragic.

Apparently the bridge I'm in now was built to unite two opposing colleges, forming Hertford College. I don't know whether that's true and neither does Wiki [*citation needed*], but I do think Oxford could do with building some more bridges for a similar effect. Having the university split into lots of little colleges might have worked when Thomas Middleton was around, but I go back to our large friend and his dated shoulder blades; the system now encourages segregation. People from Oriel don't talk to people from Balliol on principle. I don't go to Oxford, I go to Lincoln. Studying a subject I couldn't care less about.

Well I've had enough. I came here for a

reason. I'm already on my way and it's too late to catch a different train – the only way out is to jump off.

A Chinese tourist (looking notably happier than any student I've seen all day) is taking a picture of the bridge. I'll wait for her to finish – don't want to spoil the photo.

I've been here before to see what I had to do. I found out a week ago that the window panels are embedded in the stone walls like vices – there'd be no chance of me shifting them even if I joined the gym for three years... if people even have time to go to the gym round here. Perhaps this is Oxford telling me I can never escape.

It's wrong – the windows themselves open up, leaving a smallish gap between the framing. The diameter of the panels are just larger than my shoulders (thank God I don't have ones like the star of Mr Jenkins' favourite cliché).

God, could she piss about any more with that camera? *Take the bloody picture and move on – there's the Bodleian Library around the corner, that's much nicer!* I feel like shouting this at her, but it's not her fault. It's mine. No one forced me into this.

Finally, she takes the picture and walks back the way she came. I take my chance before anyone else can come, opening the window, pulling myself onto the bottom panel and resting my bum on the harsh stone window sill. It's actually angled on a downwards slope... Maybe this place wants to get rid of me after all.

I suddenly realise there's a lump in my throat and my eyes are starting to well up. I can't actually be getting upset, can I? This is my one chance to get away. Be free. I should feel ready for this...

I *am* ready. I am. I'm just getting caught up in the moment. I've thought it through enough to know that I want this.

Feet first, I squeeze through the window panel, keeping hold of the frame. It's a good job I'm skinny. "Too skinny" Mum always said...

Mum.

What would she think if - *NO! DON'T THINK ABOUT HER!*

But she – *NO!*

The breeze hits me, and the double yellow lines on the road scream at me to stop. Well your friends in the bridge weren't so bothered. They know what life is like at Oxford. They know this is my only chance to get away. Whether what's next is heaven, nothing, or something else, it's better than this restrained lie I've created for myself.

I got myself into this – it's up to me to get out of it.

I escape.

*

A light.

God that's bright.

God?

What's that beeping noise? I can hear stuff: a beeping noise.

Do I have a body?

I don't feel like me, I just feel like thoughts. How can you feel like thoughts?

This is weird. Is this heaven? Did I kill myself? If I killed myself I'd be in hell wouldn't I? Suicide is a sin isn't it?

Someone's shouting. Shut up, let me enjoy heaven for a minute – I've only just got here.

I think they're shouting "Beth!" We've not even been introduced yet and they know who I am. Impressive. Now to test out this body concept – do I have eyes? Well I can see light. So presumably. Maybe if I try to open my eyes I'll be able to... yep I can feel them. They're heavy. But wait, is that...

"Mum?" At the foot of a bed, puffy-eyed. She speaks through tears:

"You're ok! You're ok! It's... it's ok."

She has her arms round me and I can feel her wet face against mine.

"Why did you do it darling? Why did you jump off that..."

She stops herself, realising this is not the right time.

I'm in a hospital bed. People have started to rush around, coming in to see me whilst others give me drugs I do not recognise. My body still feels weird, but I'm alive.

How do I feel about that?

I'm not sure. At the moment, it just feels good to breathe. I thought I would never breathe again. To see, hear, smell. Why would I want to give this up?

Well, there *had* been a reason. And despite the huge headache I've only just become aware of, it's not too hard to remember…

Oh yes. Oxford.

I didn't like my course. But so what? That's not a reason to–

So why had I done it then?

My life had hit a dead end. I had no future.

Can that be true? Do I *have* to do a degree? Do I have to do *anything*? Can't I just enjoy the pursuit of finding something I *do* enjoy, and when I find that thing, do it as much or as little as I like?

I know I mustn't be thinking clearly – the possibility that there could be more to life than the path I've already chosen seems far too simple and logical to be something I didn't think of before. I'll have to wait until my head stops pounding to think through this properly.

A man in a white coat comes into the room. He's a doctor, with the most normal face in the world. He could be anyone.

"Hi Beth," he says. "I'm Doctor Crawford. How are you feeling?"

"I feel weird," I tell him. "My whole body feels weird. And I've got a really bad headache. But I know I'll be alright soon."

Suddenly, his face is grave. I look to the right at my mum who is curled on a chair, and her expression matches his. Tears well in her eyes.

"What?" I ask straight away. "What don't I know?"

"Beth, there's no easy way for me to tell you this," Doctor Crawford says in a soft voice. "When you... fell off the bridge, when you hit the ground, you severely damaged the lower half of your spinal cord."

No.

"Of course, we can offer you the best physiotherapy possible... but it is likely you will spend the rest of your life in a wheelchair."

My mind becomes a blur, thoughts trying to take prominence in my head and for a second I feel like I might slip back to unconsciousness. But then one thought fights its way out of the cacophony, truer than all the rest: *This is my fault.* I could find a way to blame Oxford for this if I wanted to, but *this is my fault*. It's becoming a recurring theme.

Doctor Crawford tries to fill the silence:

"Your life can still continue Beth. Your

mother tells me you study English Literature at Oxford. Well, that doesn't have to change. Books are something you'll always have, wheelchair or not."

I jumped from the Hertford Bridge, Oxford, and collided with the pavement. Astonishingly, it didn't kill me. But the subsequent words of one well-meaning doctor, trying to lighten my spirits, did.

Commentaries

This is not a necessary read, but if anyone wants to know anything that's not said explicitly in the story, here is some information on the content, writing processes and inspiration for all of the stories in *Chapter One*. While I would not call my work unoriginal, it is openly derivative in places, and below I credit all the other works I consciously got ideas from. I would urge you to read the stories themselves first or this will spoil them. I hate it when writers/directors/actors talk about their work using big words and don't actually say anything (Tim Burton...), so I'll try not to do that.

Nobody Important

I worried that some of the stories in this compilation would be too long to be considered "short stories", but this is one I don't have to worry about. *Nobody Important* was initially written as part of my "creating texts" coursework for my English Language A Level, and there was a strict word limit, so I had to make sure it was extremely concise. Had I not initially written it for college, it would no doubt have been much more fleshed out, with a bigger build up and a much longer conflict scene, but I think it benefits from the brevity. My teacher Catherine Hooley liked it, but in the drafting stage told me to change Stuart from a previous offender so that this was his first time, then the audience would have more sympathy for him. She was right of course, and the story contributed to an overall 100% coursework mark in the first year.

Only once I'd written it, did I realise it would be best to have a "style model" which influenced my story and I could compare with when writing a commentary. This was a bit of a pain, so I picked a page from *The Collector* by John Fowles (which I had never read) and tried to find ways to say it had inspired me. It was a bit tenuous, but apparently it worked as I got an overall A in English Language. Since then I have read *The Collector* and think (the first half) is fantastic – perhaps I should have read it before writing *Nobody Important* and it could have been even better.

After the coursework deadline, it was entered into Penguin Books' "A Story For Our Time" writing competition in the Daily Telegraph, which asked for short stories that reflected the contemporary world. The winner would be chosen by John le Carré, author of *Tinker, Tailor, Soldier, Spy.* The judges shortlisted *Nobody Important* as one of the six best stories, describing it as "a modern day parable about the dangers of internet chat rooms and online relationships, with a fresh and clever twist." Although it was never supposed to be a caveat of these very real dangers, if it helps anyone think differently about it, I will take all credit for saving your life. The winner of the competition was announced just after the wedding of Prince William and Kate Middleton and happened to come from the same college as the new Duchess of Cambridge, providing a timely angle for the reports of her success; what a nice coincidence! I'm not bitter I swear…

Jack Downs, an up-and-coming director from Leeds, has recently shown an interest in adapting *Nobody Important* into a short film.

Interested in the psychological thriller genre, Jack is always looking for new material and was a fan of the story. The film could potentially be produced in the summer of this year, and I'd be involved in the translation from prose to screenplay.

I was originally going to call the whole book *Nobody Important* to reflect how, at the moment, I'm nobody important in the current writer's landscape. When I realised though that the main purpose of the compilation was to throw up some premises to see what people might like to see developed, I thought *Chapter One* was more appropriate.

Subjective Groaning

Subjective Groaning is the kind of piece I find easiest to write: a monologue-style hyperbolic extension of my own thoughts, combined with dialogue, action and witticisms. I could write them all day, but I know they're not everyone's cup of tea so I didn't want to fill this book with them. It was originally written as part of my A Level English Literature coursework where we had to write a piece inspired by a book. As was the case with *Nobody Important,* I had written the piece, entitled *Subjective Groanings* (notice the plural) too early and my teacher Louise Tipping then told me to go and "get inspired" by Hunter S. Thompson's *Fear And Loathing In Las Vegas* (hence the novel's appearance in the story), which she thought my piece could be linked to in the commentary I had to write. I could not get into the book at all, but the exam board seemed to buy that it had inspired me, and it contributed to an overall A grade in English Literature.

At this point, the piece only consisted of the first internal monologue, up until when he meets his dad. We were asked at the beginning of A2 Theatre Studies to write and perform a monologue in front of the students who had just started the subject that year, to show them what the course entailed. I converted the monologue into a performance for this live, unsuspecting audience. I decided to go all-out and fully physicalise the zombies, which went down quite well (even with my drama-sceptical mate Nod who turned up to watch), and I think the performance was unanimously appreciated (except for almost biting a girl in the front row, but we shan't dwell on that). The real benefit from it though was that it seemed to have sparked my interest in the character again. I continued writing *Subjective Groanings*, adding all the concrete scenes in, and it was finished in less than two weeks. The writing process was not one I usually follow – just continuing writing without a clear sense of where I wanted to go with the story, but I think it provided some interesting storytelling and ideas in this instance.

I think it would be wrong for me not to say the story was inspired by Brian K. Vaughn's *Y: The Last Man,* one of the best things I have ever read. It is similar in its use of juxtaposition between dystopian and humorous tones and the refreshingly genuine nature of a pop-culture-obsessed protagonist. Although there are things that annoy me about the ending of *Y,* I like the unexpected poignancy it carries, and so I read the epilogue again before writing the final sequence of (what was then titled) *Subjective Groanings* to try and emulate some of that. I think my ending is more pessimistic, but this is something I wanted since studying Shakespeare at a summer school at Oxford:

As much as I love Shakespeare, sometimes I am doubtful that he meant to do everything people say he did. At Oxford, I found many critics say that at the end of *The Tempest*, although the characters are optimistic about their new future, the audience are meant to doubt things will go well for them because of the turbulent past they share. As far as I can see, Shakespeare gives no clue that this is what he actually meant for us to think, ending on an otherwise optimistic speech from Prospero. I wanted to end the story with an optimistic voice, but make it obvious that the future will be dire – Andy has become an outlaw through his own actions. He has made a future with his daughter impossible by running away with her from the hospital, and the final line could suggest he knows the delusion won't last long. I put the last line in the present tense so that the readers imagine he is currently on the run and hopefully worry what will happen to him in the future.

I also think that the story must have been

influenced by the recent works of Robert Kirkman. While I am not a zombie obsessive like Andy, I loved both *Marvel Zombies* and *The Walking Dead*, especially the latter which, whilst inspiring a consistently exciting TV series, is an amazing read. I eagerly await the new book every year, if only because (unlike properties owned by big companies, such as Spider-Man or Batman), absolutely anything can and does happen. I'd urge you to check it out!

Since the success of the initial drama performance and completing the story, the opening has been re-adapted into part of a half hour piece of theatre which contributed to 20% of my A Level Theatre Studies course and an overall A* Grade. Our group devised a production called *Mental Space* showing a range of mindsets from one person with multiple personality disorder. The personality I represented was our good friend Andy. Initially a series of monologues, we fragmented the whole piece to make it more thought provoking, with the zombie obsessive being the only one that remained intact, acting as an introduction to the performance. There were some slight changes from the story to make it fit the overall performance, for example the conversation he had with the omniscient narrator, in which I gave him the line "you and your subjective groanings" for my own amusing homage to the story I'd written. Ollie Winnington, who said the line, always said "groaning" instead of "groanings" and he's right – it does make much more sense, so I changed the name of my story. Thanks Ollie. The rest of the cast enhanced the piece by acting as zombies and various other characters, and I'd love to adapt the whole thing into a drama or radio performance one day.

There are other smaller things to note about *Subjective Groaning*: The very first line, which provided the basis for the whole thing, was a question that my old drama teacher, Mike Rees, once asked me, and without that conversation I probably wouldn't have written this story at all – thanks Mike. Andy's use of gas and air at the birth of his child and the way in which Christie nearly breaks his arm during the birth was inspired by John Sullivan's hilarious *Only Fools and Horses* episode: *Three Men, a Woman and a Baby*. The "my spider-senses weren't particularly tingly today" line caused me lots of grief – in the comics, all letters are capitals so I didn't know whether spider-sense should be capitalised or not. I got in touch with the current Spider-Man writer, a fantastic guy named Dan Slott who kindly advised me to keep it all lower case. Finally, Andy's desire to have his life filmed when he does something awesome is something I have to admit to thinking often myself.

Bubbles

There is a strong implication throughout *Bubbles* that "Michael" is a certain Canadian swinger who we all know and love (or we do if we have any taste in music). I never use his surname because I don't want it to be a "Michael Bublé" story rather than one about an eventful night in the life of a celebrity. Plus I don't want Michael thinking it's supposed to be biographical and suing me when he buys his copy. I've just used his surname though so that's probably void now, but I think he's a great guy so I probably shouldn't worry too much. For all intents and purposes: yes, it is him I'm writing about, but it is not true. I don't think...

The story's title is an allusion to Michael's surname and the bubbles in the Jacuzzi. The plot came to me whilst I was at work listening to the singer in question and by the time I had finished my shift, was completely plotted. I never usually plot solidly until I have a finished structure like that – things either appear in my head fully formed or fall into place over a period of time, so after a rigorous mental "plotting" session, I was quite proud that I had consciously structured the story from start to finish. Or at least I thought I had; it had originally ended with a nice security guard helping Michael and slipping him quietly away, but when it came to writing it, a high-speed action-packed chase scene with the butler seemed much more entertaining.

The story takes place in the middle of Michael's *Crazy Love Tour*, between the Manchester and Birmingham dates in October 2010 (he wasn't married then, hence the "engaged to a supermodel" line). The set that he performs at the party is the genuine set list he performed back then. Sadly I did not go to watch the tour, although I have managed to blag me and my girlfriend VIP tickets to one of his shows in London this year, so I am extremely excited. I'll bring a copy of *Bubbles* for him just in case he gets kidnapped afterwards and needs something to read in the car.

I tried to keep Spider-Man out of *Chapter One* as much as I could as I know not everyone is as madly in love with him as I am (explicit references anyway – any Spidey fanatics will be able to see his influence throughout the whole book). However, I couldn't resist putting the webbed mask on Michael's head in the taxi – Bublé has done an excellent cover of the classic Spider-Man theme tune which can be found during the end credits of *Spider-Man 2*, and the image of him wearing the mask is something that satisfies me greatly. That was simply self-indulgence I'm afraid.

Fear's Touch

The whole point of *Chapter One* was to try out different styles and genres to see which had a positive response, so a horror/thriller story was inevitable. I wanted *Fear's Touch* to be an attempt at the genre where you never really see the subject of fear, an effective technique which has been used in "watch once" films such as *The Blair Witch Project*. Some people are really into that kind of thing, while some just find it frustrating, and if the latter applies to you, then I apologise for the cliff-hanger ending. While it is presumably the hand of Joseph Fear on Becky's paralysed shoulder at the end of the story, which would explain its very title, maybe it's someone else? Perhaps it is Josh's hand on her shoulder, recovered and come to save her? Or a police officer? The resurrected body of Andrea Fear? Alice's zombie body, looking for its head...? OK, it's not the last one, but only I know who it really is –insert evil laugh–

Whether *Fear's Touch* is a successful thriller is open to debate. It's true that the build-up is very quick and transparent, but unlike full length horror books or films, it's a short story – you can't have a really long introduction. I wanted to get straight to the action, which is of course the most interesting and exciting part. The escaped murderer exposition, hearing snapping sounds behind them and the graveyard setting could all be seen as clichés, but I like to think I'm just embracing the conventions of the genre. And hey, at least I didn't make it rain...

The idea for this dark story unbelievably came to me in sunny Majorca. I was about to read *Blacklands* by Belinda Bauer. The cover and the blurb led to my prediction that at some point in the book, the main character would fall down a dug-up grave and would not be able to get out. I was quite sure this would happen as the book went on, and was looking forward to it. Although I did enjoy *Blacklands* a lot, my prediction was wrong and I was left with this image that I had wanted to see happen which hadn't. Then, realising that I was not copying anything but my own ideas, I decided to use this prediction in one of my own stories and the rest, as they say, is history.

The first line from *Fear's Touch* is the penultimate line, spoken by Mary Jane Watson, from my own first personal "horror" experience. *The Alien Costume* trilogy from the fantastic Spider-Man cartoon series in 1994 was the first time a form of entertainment had made me genuinely terrified. I had it on video and my mum threatened to sell it if I didn't watch it, so I did, and loved it although it did scare me senseless. I now have it on DVD and still watch it, although it's safe to say I don't find it scary anymore. But I just wanted to stick a line from that in.

The line "there were more shadows than there were objects" was also one I knew I had to put in *Chapter One* somewhere, and this story seemed like the obvious choice. I came up with that line in primary school which led to much appraise off my teacher Mr Bachelor who went on to tell following pupils (including my brother of three years younger) about how subtly suggestive it was. I don't know now if it's really that good, but I was proud of it at the time and thought it should be in here.

I think the use of sound is integral in *Fear's Touch*, through both silence and otherwise. I read all of the stories in *Chapter One* aloud as part of the proofreading process (and because my flatmates needed another excuse to think I'm crazy) and this is easily the one I enjoyed reading aloud the most. I liked holding the tension in my voice throughout, and if there was ever an audiobook version, I wouldn't let anyone else be the one to read it. I'm prepared for a film version when it comes to sound too, having written a piece of music that lends well to Becky's search for Alice through the graveyard.

Die Entartung

I shouldn't take any credit for *Die Entartung*. I was literally just doing my civil duty, letting the world know the truth about Adolf Hitler. His brain was transferred into a monkey's body before his "death" at the end of the Second World War, and I was just telling the story as it was. It's the second story in *Chapter One* about a real person, but as Hitler is long gone and was an evil maniac, I don't think I'll have too many legal issues with this one. But you never know…

An advert for *The Change-Up* in 2011 described it as "the body-swap to end all body-swaps". While it did look funny, to me it seemed to be just two ordinary guys swapping bodies... nothing too original. I thought I could go one better. Or ten. I was in Majorca and had just thought of the idea for *Fear's Touch* and several other unpublished stories, and felt I was in the middle of a creative streak. I remember chilling on a lilo coming up with ideas for a body-swap to actually end all body-swaps, which started off with Henry VIII's brain getting transferred into a hamster, but I thought that was quite limited. Then I decided I wanted to do something with Hitler and really ridicule him posthumously.

At first I thought a penguin would be brilliant, but a monkey makes it easier for him to move, and therefore for the plot to advance. If he was a penguin he'd just angrily waddle around and that'd be it. Plus, not only is it thought that the surname "Hitler" originates from "one who lives in a hut", which becomes appropriate in this zoo, but a monkey is *slightly* more believable because we're so similar biologically. I know that it's pretty farfetched, but I'm an English student not a scientist. If I ever do anything in a similar vein I'll try and throw even more big words in to cover myself, a technique probably not invented by, but exploited by Stan Lee. But no matter how I got there, having Hitler in a monkey's body was never going to be believable so why bother picking apart the science? Is that not like watching *Toy Story* and saying: "But toys can't talk"?

If not scientifically realistic, the story is as historically accurate as I could possibly make it. I made sure that it could fit into Hitler's timeline, with location, character and small references for avid historians. Blondi was Hitler's German shepherd, and I nearly used her instead of the cat in the demonstration, but I didn't think Haase would be cheeky enough to use him. Haase himself was Hitler's physician, who he thought very highly of. I even made sure the story correlated to the official floor plan of the Führerbunker. There are lots of other details that I won't bother mentioning here, but if I mention a specific person or place in relation to Hitler, you know that they did at some point exist.

The monkey escape from the zoo was also a real event. In July 1956, forty five rhesus monkeys escaped from the Tierpark Hagenbeck Zoo and ran wild in Hamburg. I thought I could tie the two things together, and this gave me the idea for the 11 year time gap that I never planned to have but I think works really well.

The opening after the time-jump with David was written as part of my Writing Fiction course with the Open University, and builds nicely into the revelation that he has transformed into a monkey, rather than just presenting the reader with it straight away.

The motivation of the characters is obviously not quite so accurate. I don't believe Haase would have done anything other than work at the casualty station, but I preferred using him than inventing a crackpot scientist as it means Hitler would be close enough to trust him. I also don't think the real Hitler would have genuinely taken a serum only tested on a cat and a monkey, but he knew he was going to die anyway, so you never know. Of course, it is possible that Hitler *does* die and his version of hell (because let's face it, that's where he'd end up) is living as an animal who can't voice his opinions. Or that he *does* move into the unconscious Aryan but everything after that is a drug-induced dream. Or that he dies and is

283

reincarnated as a monkey. We can't be sure.

I know some people will turn their noses up at *Die Entartung*. My friends did many a time whilst I was writing it and poorly explaining what it was about, which is fair enough – if you explain it, it does sound stupid. At the end of the day, it's a bit of fun. Yes it's written in a serious style, but I think it's hard not to when dealing with serious history like WWII. I think that just adds to the comic effect though when juxtaposed with what's happening, but I may be wrong.

You've probably realised by now that this story is the inspiration for Hannah's brilliant cover image – a rhesus macaque in Hitler's uniform. Obviously the image is symbolic in that he never wears the uniform whilst being a monkey, but literal in that he actually does turn into monkey and it does not represent something figurative like the devolution of man. The subtle moustache on the monkey was hard work – we knew it needed one, but it looked silly with a full black Hitler moustache and had to blend in so it could just have been part of the monkey's hair and didn't look ridiculous.

Hannah did a great job.

"Die Entartung", pronounced "dee-en-tar-tung" is German for "the devolution". Thanks to Chris Lloyd and Emma Freudenthal for translation assistance – translating one word is harder than you might think when there are nine German words for that one English word on first glance.

When Hitler first wakes up after the body-swap (before the reader knows exactly what has happened to him) he is in the birdcage that Haase kept Benno the monkey in. The soldier shakes him from that cage, which brings him to his senses and gets him running wild through the bunker. Why would the soldier do that? Because he's cruel. It is unclear how Hitler gets to the zoo, but presumably one of the soldiers made sure he was taken care of and transported to the Tierpark.

Notice how Hitler and Haase are referred to by their surnames before the body-swap and then afterwards Hitler is called Adolf. This represents how he is less of a man now that he's a monkey, until the last line when his surname indicates he has found himself again.

The inspiration for the initial body/mind swap with the cat and the monkey was probably the use of polyjuice potion in *Harry Potter and the Chamber of Secrets*, as I imagine their skin bubbling just as Harry and Ron's do when they transform into Crabbe and Goyle. So thanks to everyone who had an input in that.

The pointed brackets around the speech indicate that it is translated, in this instance from German. I only knew myself what those marks were used for other than "more or less" because this same translation representation is used a lot in comic books.

I don't know what the response will be for this story. I thought writing a story with Hitler as the main character would be quite controversial, but my mum and Hannah really enjoyed it so that's a good start. If there is enough of a positive response for a continuation, we could see Hitler try and find out what happened to his original body, try and find Hasse to ask what went wrong, and start communicating with other humans to build up an army and establish the New Order. How possible would this be in his body? Time will

286

(possibly) tell. If it is not continued, we can assume that he has completely deluded himself at the end of *Die Entartung* and his monkey restraints mean he fails miserably. It is possible though that if it is continued, the events will be large enough that they just can't fit into our real timeline like this short story does.

Letting Go

If you didn't get this story, here's a very blunt explanation: A man goes to spread his wife's ashes with his daughter. On the way, the surroundings are personified so they seem to be alive, distracting him from the recent tragedy. Then he thinks back to a time with his wife, and realises she is the only true form of life, recalling how he promised to remember her that way. The red butterfly (notice it is the same colour as his wife's dress) allows them to accept her death and say goodbye.

A story which appeared fully formed in my head from nothing, *Letting Go* was the one I was most wary about including in *Chapter One*, knowing that the poetic style would make it stick out from the rest. It's so poetic in fact that I have converted it into a poem, which uses capitalisation to further personify the surroundings at the beginning of their story.

Despite it being very different to the rest I am proud of *Letting Go*, and I think some of my past English teachers who read it will be too. Every word is carefully selected and I like to think I elicit a fair share of emotion in the story, as opposed to a more action-based one like *Bubbles*. There are several subtleties inside it that can be picked up on as well, such as the double meaning of "so I let go," the implication that his wife may have known she was ill by what she says on the cruise, and the fact that if the cruise was six months ago, it is likely the butterfly is out of season, making its presence even more poignant.

"Daddy look it's a butterfly" is a line from one of my favourite films, *I Am Legend* (only really made relevant if you watch the alternate ending), and for some reason found its way into *Letting Go* as soon as I had thought of the idea. Although my story is not otherwise linked to the movie, I felt the line had somehow inspired the whole story so I named the speaker of it

"Marley" after the speaker in the film.

Over The Rainbow

Over The Rainbow is the culmination of a series of ideas that were kicking around in my head for quite a long time. It started at a workshop day at Manchester Metropolitan University that we went to with college (and met Britain's wonderful Poet Laureate, Carol Ann Duffy). One of the workshops was on scriptwriting. I didn't learn a thing about scriptwriting it has to be said, but as part of the character creation process, the teacher gave everyone a shoe and told us all to create a character who might wear this shoe. Mine was a red pump. I pretended it was a ruby slipper, and soon had a story where a woman had to steal a slipper from someone she hated who had the same role as her but in a bigger theatre, which I thought might be quite amusing.

I never actually started writing until about five months later when I had to write an opening for a story as part of my Writing Fiction module with the Open University. My tutor Maidy did some drafting with me, and helped me re-structure the introduction. The first conversation with her Mum, (which I changed from being with her friend Raquel to establish the character of her mother before the final scene) was also edited as part of that course.

Over the next month or so I finished it off, using it as an excuse to watch *The Wizard of Oz* and *Bridget Jones's Diary* with the beautiful Hannah Williams to try and get some inspiration. I like to think that this contributed to making the early stages of our relationship a success, and the year I have spent with her since has been simply brilliant.

This story must be heavily influenced by my time performing in *Peter Pan* and *The Wizard Of Oz* at the Lowry theatre in Manchester, alongside actors such as Paul Nicholas, Susie Blake and Justin Moorhouse. The actors' names (but not personalities) for the larger performance of *The Wizard of Oz* in the story are the same as they were in mine, and it was that theatre that I pictured when describing on and back stage. I didn't want to use a real theatre for the crap one as I don't want to slag any theatres off, and the only bad one I know of is not in

Manchester.

The wine anecdote at the start is half autobiographical in that I sent an email with questions about studying English and Creative Writing at the "Birmingham of University." I wasn't expecting an offer after that, but I did actually get one. The flashback of Sally falling through an imaginary wall and walking round to get back in is one that just fell into my head when watching *Seasons Greetings* by Alan Ayckbourn (my favourite playwright) at the Theatre Clwyd, although as far as I was aware nothing similar really happened in the performance.

Over The Rainbow was an attempt at writing a story that women would enjoy – "chick lit" if you like. While I do not dislike it, I think I found it hard because it is different from what I am used to, and because of this I would probably say it is the weakest story in the book. I wouldn't rush and write a similar thing anytime soon, but if you *did* enjoy it, I'm glad.

Next Genesis

I would be a fool to deny this story being

heavily influenced by my continuous following of Marvel's multi-layered X-Men franchise over the latter half of my life. The significant difference is that the powers developed in my story are the result of an illegal government programme – invention, not mutation. The President's speech is an homage to the announcement of the mutant cure in the *X-Men: The Last Stand* movie, which in turn was inspired by Joss Whedon's wonderful *Gifted* storyline in *Astonishing X-Men.* I am not ashamed of how much inspiration I took from X-Men, because I feel I am doing something significantly different. And X-Men's supposedly a rip-off of *Doom Patrol* anyway…

Evie and Adam were originally possible new creations for X-Men should I ever have the honour of contributing to the ongoing story. I developed them into two independent characters for two separate stories, both of which were lacking in a substantial plot, so I merged them into what we have now.

Evie's powers are of course not my design, with telepaths such as Jean Grey, Professor X and Emma Frost littering the X-Men universe.

The way in which she discovers her powers however, was something I quite liked (thinking the other person was the mutate), although it is likely to be influenced by the telepathic affair between Emma Frost and the married Cyclops in Grant Morrison's excellent *New X-Men* story. I also think the nature of the telepathy comes across different here than in X-Men – the use of prose instead of visuals allows a more elaborate description of something that I don't think could be captured in a 2D image.

Adam is a concept that came to me fully formed – without any thinking I had a character who could use reflective surfaces to transport himself across space. I searched the many X-Men databases and could not find a character with similar powers, so hopefully he is original and I won't be receiving a visit from the plagiarism police.

The story was only titled *Next Genesis* weeks before this book went to print. In the template copy, and for the whole time I was writing it, it was called *Reflective Thoughts* because of the nature of both of their powers, but I just didn't think it was a striking enough title. *Next Genesis* seemed more appropriate because obviously it is about the possible next generation of humans. The allusion to the first chapter of the bible is intentional (notice how the two main characters' names are a parallel of Adam and Eve), and the word "next" could imply this is set in our future, acting as the opposite of a traditional bible. It is also an allusion to *Second Genesis,* the *X-Men* story by Len Wein and Dave Cockrum which completely revamped the team and introduced Wolverine, Storm, Nightcrawler and Colossus, making the comic much more diverse and interesting.

Although it is the longest story in *Chapter One*, I consider *Next Genesis* to be very fast paced in that a lot happens in a (relatively) small amount of words. It's a good representation of the kind of thing I like to read – a nice balance between character dilemma and romance with action and politics. The one issue I have with it is that it reads too much like a "Chapter One" rather than a contained short story, and sorry if the abruptness of the ending annoyed you, but one of the reasons for this book is to introduce things that could be expanded upon. I thought about having Evie take control of the helicopter pilot at the end and send the rocket into the complex, but this seemed too abrupt/violent (there could be many innocent people inside) and a bit of an injustice for what the story could potentially become.

Although the ending is ambiguous as to whether they survive or not (they could have been pulled into the water by the rocket or by Adam's power of teleporting through reflective surfaces, of which the water is one of), if the story has a positive response I will continue it and show that they are still alive. Two very different people, they would help each other come to terms with the powers they never asked for and work together to try and bring down a disgusting (government?) programme. If the response does not encourage a continuation, it is up to you whether Adam and Evie died, although the ellipsis at the end certainly implies their story does not finish here. Maybe Adam managed to teleport himself but not Evie? Who knows.

The banker who stands up to Adam is inspired by the "what do you believe in" banker in the first scene of Christopher Nolan's *The Dark Knight*. I thought it was great how a banker actually cared that much about his bank, whether he owned it or just worked there.

The Return

This was one of those stories that seemed to appear fully formed from nowhere, (and was written such a long time ago) so I am unsure of its origins. Perhaps it was something I dreamt/daydreamt about? I wish I knew where it came from then I could go back and get something else.

I used an early draft of *The Return* for my GCSE English Language exam, in which everyone had to write a story. My fantastic teacher, Sarah du Plessis, suggested that instead of Robert going back to his house simply to see the fairies out of curiosity, (which is what it was at the time), there should be a more important motivation. So, for the exam, I used the idea that his son was being bullied, so he went to get the fairies to make his son happier. In the exam we were given five titles to choose from to write a story, although everyone had memorised a story or two which would hopefully fit into one of the five given titles. I had two versions of *The Return* ready – one was in case the only title I could use was something like "The Disappointment," and it had Robert finding an empty clearing at the end. I never liked that one though, and was glad to be rid of it after the GCSE had finished. I memorised the whole thing word for word, regurgitated it in the exam, and came out with a high A*.

Nearly two years later, upon being asked to take part in The Portico Prize For Young Writers (of which I ended up winning the non-fiction award), I dug *The Return* out and started to rework it for the fiction category of the competition. Although I didn't change much other than the wording, my time with the mentors at the Portico Library in Manchester made me realise that at the end of the day, the fairies would obviously not be able to stop William being bullied, and if Robert cared that much he could go round to their houses and confront them, so I knew that I needed a new reason for him returning. It was my mum that suggested I make it so William was ill, and I think it works a lot better now. I'm always amazed by people's different responses to the new version though: I think it says a lot about a person whether they find it "sweet" because of the seemingly happy ending or "sad" because William is of course dying and the fairies can (presumably) not do anything to stop that. Either way, I think it's pretty moving, and one of the pieces I'm most proud of.

Although it is usually to my distaste when stories are not given to us on a plate so we know exactly what everything is and what everything looks like, I am happy with the ending of *The Return*. I like how it doesn't explicitly say what he has returned to, whilst having enough information to make it clear that it is some kind of fairy-like creature, and allowing the audience to picture their own mini-paradise for Robert. The clues are there throughout the story, from the "fairy trapped in a jar" simile in the second line, to the image: "gliding across the water […], the tips of his toes his only body part getting wet," which is meant to be the creatures carrying him through the air above the pond, although obviously at this stage of the story you wouldn't know that yet.

A student from Cambridge said that it "reads like a first chapter." If this is the case, it is in the right place. I'm not sure if I do consider it to be a first chapter though; it's been a finished article for so many years now that I think a continuation would be unnatural. I have not yet thought of a "Chapter Two" which does justice to *The Return* (in fact, everything I have thought of has just been downright weird), and unless I ever do think of something, it's staying as it is.

Bridge of Sighs

Bridge Of Sighs is written in a monologue style that I find worryingly easy to write – find something for someone to moan about and imagine I feel as strongly about it as they do. It was written when I went to Oxford University on a UNIQ Summer School, studying English Literature for a week. While Beth's extreme views do not completely reflect my own at the time, the summer school did open my eyes to how I felt about what the academic world considers to be "literature." When I raised my opinions on this, the phrase "standing on the shoulders of giants" was the response I got, hence it's inclusion in the story. (And it's true, it is one of Oasis's weaker albums.) I had a great week at Oxford, and it was beneficial in showing me that the university, and English Literature at degree level, are not for me. I put the story last as a bit of a manifesto in a way, stating that I'm attempting to try and move away from traditionalist views of literature and education. I am currently studying at Lancaster University, and I enjoy how relevant it is.

The bridge at Hertford College in Oxford is known as the Bridge of Sighs. Obviously that, and the nature of how Beth is feeling, is where the story's name came from. I wrote it sitting opposite the bridge and on the bridge itself. How I managed to get on such an exclusive bridge could have become a story in itself, but I don't want to get myself arrested when this book goes to print.

Being on the bridge caused me to realise that the panels in the windows themselves would have prevented anybody from jumping out of one, how I had originally planned Beth's attempted suicide. I panicked then as the story had pretty much been written, and tourists below (some Chinese and messing with cameras) were watching me pace back and forth trying to find a way for Beth to kill herself authentically. I eventually found the window panel she slides out of, but I knew that I couldn't fit through... how convenient that the character I created is so slim.

The story is written in the present tense as it makes the stream of consciousness more believable and adds a brutal immediacy to the suicide attempt. Whereas *Subjective Groaning* switches to the present tense for the final line, this changes to the past tense to create a reflective and defeated mood.

Beth is named after a girl I met at Oxford, Beth Williams. I don't often name characters after people I have met, and the real Beth is a history student at Nottingham who (I hope) is not in the least bit suicidal, so the only similarity there is her Christian name. The doctor is named after the lovely Doctor Mariah Crawford in the 1994 *Spider-Man* cartoon for no other reason than I liked her character.

About The Author

Only 19 years of age, Simon has always been a keen writer. He had his first published short story in 2008 – *Silver Skin* in a compilation book called *The Hat Never Comes Off*, and *Chapter One* is his first fully-published book.

As well as fictional writing, he has written news stories and colloquial articles for newspapers and magazines respectively, and was granted The Portico Prize for Non-Fiction in 2011 for a political opinion piece.

Simon left the County High School Leftwich in 2010 with The Rotary Award for Academic Achievement and Service to School, and sat his A Levels at Sir John Deane's College. He is currently studying English Language and Creative Writing in his first year at Lancaster University, under an academic scholarship.

In his spare time, Simon enjoys playing the cornet and the trumpet in various different bands, and has no hesitation in admitting his obsession for reading Spider-Man comic books.